SHAPES IN THE DARK

William Jackson is a British author of queer horror fiction. His writing explores the themes of oppression, the seductiveness of evil and the corruption hidden within beauty. He cites his influences as James Herbert, Dennis Wheatley and Fred Mustard Stewart.

Jackson is the new master of gay horror, reaching to the heart of the reader's deepest fears - then deftly twisting his pen. His stories have been described as *Hammer Horror for the 21st Century*.

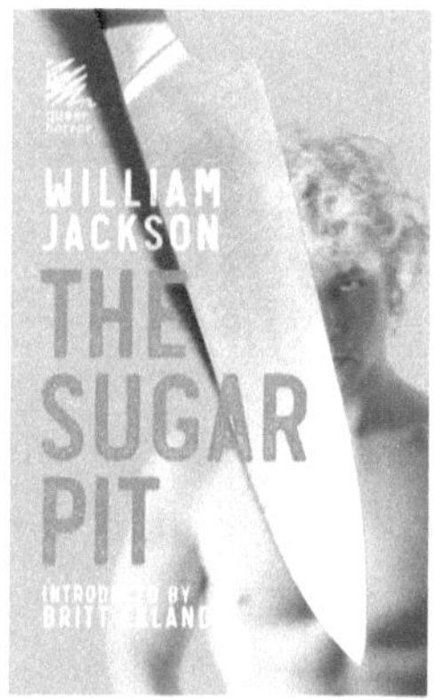

Devil's Rock is the bleakest lighthouse station off the Cornish coast. A lonely rock that locals say is haunted. That's why they call it 'Satan's Lamp'.

Young Jabe Walker, a rookie keeper, is plagued by nightmares of his abusive father - the father Jabe killed when he was just ten years old.

Now it is the 15th of October 1987 and one of the most violent storms in history is about to strike the English coast. On this night Jabe is forced to confront his violent past.

London. England. 1988. A time of anti-gay laws, queer-bashing and 'traditional family values'.

Jack Huntley is a thirty-something family man with a respectable job. And a secret. He cruises London's gay bars looking for sex with younger men.

Billy Soanes is a college student. Out, proud, hot-blooded and obsessive.

Jack and Billy begin an affair. When Jack wants out, their relationship becomes more volatile... and more violent.

WILLIAM JACKSON

SHAPES IN THE DARK

INTRODUCED BY CAROLINE MUNRO

Cambridge
Queer Press

First published in 2021 by the Cambridge Queer Press, an imprint of MFco Ltd. Unit 4 City Limits, Danehill, Reading RG6 4UP, UK.

ISBN 978-1-912622-33-7

Text is set in Didot, 11pt on 15pt.

CONTENTS

Introduction — 7

Out of Water — 13

Clem — 23

Children of Sirius — 33

Forbidden — 43

45 Minutes — 57

Hairy Tale — 67

Expiry Date — 77

Run! — 89

Beneath the Surface — 97

My Funny Valentine — 105

The Muddlers — 117

Possession — 127

Black Shuck — 135

New, Improved — 145

Prowler — 155

The Swedish House — 163

Echoes — 173

Charlie — 183

INTRODUCTION

Caroline Munro: Writing an introduction to this extraordinary book seemed a natural fit - William Jackson's otherworldly stories have been described as *Hammer Horror for the 21st Century* - my own journey with Hammer began in 1971 when I had the great privilege of working with three masters of the genre: Christopher Lee, Peter Cushing and Vincent Price. All screen icons in their own right.

My love of horror began in those early years. I remember clearly being on set at Pinewood Studios - a recreation of a deconsecrated church - for the making of *Dracula A.D. 1972*. Because Dracula transcends time, the character is a fantastic vehicle for exploring passion, lust and fear as it has been experienced through the ages. The moment I saw

Christopher Lee in full Count attire - his red eyes glaring down at me, his long black cloak billowing amidst the dry ice rising around him - I found it easy to identify with my character, Laura Bellows. I was delighted with the emotional connection I felt and that was the 'lightbulb moment' that made me realise I wanted to pursue acting seriously. Working with Christopher gave me experience and cemented my relationship with Hammer Films. I was entranced from that day forward with all things Gothic; the style, the allure and the mystique surrounding the genre.

The Hammer Horror film company, founded in 1934, is one of the oldest film companies in the world. Since the beginning, it has transported audiences to different time periods. William Jackson sets his stories in different eras, creating detailed pictures of different lives and times. Then he delves under the surface of the everyday to explore what really lies beneath.

His writing is immensely visual. I felt I had stepped into eighteen different worlds. The narratives are hauntingly gentle and spine-chilling in equal measure. Bewitching and erotic. What a heady mix of emotions and feelings!

Out of Water resonates so much with me as I grew up by the sea. I've often walked along a deserted beach on my own, early in the morning or when the sun is setting, magical times. You see something way off in the distance and you are drawn towards it. I would often collect things from the beach to take home, like a beautiful piece of wood - from a shipwreck, perhaps - your imagination takes off.

This is the situation Matt finds himself in as he walks along the shore. This kind and nurturing soul, who has chosen to live close to nature, finds his life changed totally by an unexpected encounter on the beach. I was as absorbed by the story as Matt is by his chance meeting.

45 Minutes also explores the allure of the unknown but, unlike *Out of Water* with its natural setting, this story is steeped in urban hedonism and much darker enticements. It's a tale of power, corruption, pain, copious amounts of money and every sexual encounter Pete, our protagonist, could desire. He obtained these dubious pleasures by inheriting a dark but enticing gift that gave him seven magical years of pure indulgence.

But with the gift came equal amounts of pleasure and deep, controlling, oppressive pain. There is an urgency to this story, hence the title. The story's settings are beautifully evoked from the heat of Spain to the ever-present cold of winter creeping in as night falls and midnight approaches.

I have known people living this kind of lifestyle. The story raises questions about what living well really means, and explores the value of a life that burns brightly, even though it may be short. A shorter life-less-ordinary, packed with all your heart's desires, is enticing to some, but hedonistic pleasures can lose their allure, no longer providing the gratification that once seemed so attractive. Pete makes a deal with the Devil but, as this tale shows us, the cosmos always seeks balance.

All of the stories in the collection lull you into a false sense of security, then pivot abruptly, trapping you, more often than not, in inescapable mayhem.

Some of the stories have satisfyingly conclusive endings. Others leave you to use your imagination, which is always interesting as no two people have exactly the same thoughts. It would be strange if we all thought with one accord, rather than making up our own minds and having an open discussion about our impressions.

Shapes in the Dark left me feeling stirred emotionally, moved and on edge at the same time. I am so glad I was sitting at home reading the collection! A Gothic streak is woven through the tales, taking me back to wonderful times telling stories like these myself. *Shapes in the Dark* would easily translate to the magic of the silver screen and I would be excited to see that.

We all have an innate fear of, and curiosity for, the forbidden. I remember as a child sneaking down to watch black and white films, unbeknownst to my parents, and seeing things that both thrilled and frightened me.

William Jackson's narratives flux and flow, examining the nature of evil and at the same time acknowledging the grey areas in human experience, which keeps the reader intrigued, wanting to turn the next page. I found myself expecting the unexpected. As humans we are naturally intrigued by the beauty of the unknown, and the *Shapes in the Dark*.

Caroline Munro

'The boy's hair was silver-blond,
his skin pale as pearl.'

OUT OF WATER

A warm breeze scattered clouds of sand across the shore. Pearl-tipped combers ran hard against the beach, drawing up the wave-wet shingle as they retreated. Matt walked absent-mindedly, swallowed up by the vast emptiness of the beach and its wildness. He noticed something lying at the wave line, tangled and stranded, unmoving in the day's dying light. He thought it might be a resting seal - or a dead one. As he got closer, he saw its human nakedness. And he began to run.

He bent over the still figure. A boy, probably in his late teens. Matt cradled him gently. The boy's hair was silver-blond, like steel, his skin pale as pearl, catching the soft hues of early evening. His jaw was strong and dimpled. His face was young, heroic even. Matt stroked the boy's cheek to rouse him and he opened his large dark eyes.

'Are you all right? What happened? Were you out swimming?'

The boy just looked at him and blinked. He was trembling.

'Let's get you into the warm.'

By the time they got to the beach house, the shoreline had greyed behind them and the embers of the day were glowing faintly at the horizon. Matt laid the boy on the bed and covered him with a blanket. He made hot tea and the boy drank it eagerly.

'Careful,' Matt said, 'or you'll burn your mouth. What's your name?'

The boy smiled, 'I don't know.'

'You don't know your own name? Have you been in an accident? What were you doing out there on the beach?'

'I was in the water. I love the water.'

'Where are your clothes?'

'I don't have any.'

'You don't have any clothes? I think you may have taken a knock on the head, sunshine. Maybe we should get you looked at.'

'No,' the boy grasped Matt's wrist. 'No. Please, don't. I'm okay.'

'All right, but let me get you something to eat.'

Matt gave the boy a tee shirt, socks and sweatpants. The sweatpants were slightly too big and

Matt pulled the drawstring tight to keep them from sliding down the boy's narrow hips. They went into the kitchen.

'What's the last thing you remember before I found you?' Matt heated passata and put some rigatoni on to boil.

'Swimming to the shore,' the boy said. 'I wanted to see the shore.'

'Nothing before that?'

'No.'

'And you don't know your name?'

The boy shook his head. There was something oddly unworldly about him.

'Well, I think I'm going to call you Dylan. It's a Welsh name. Means *son of the sea*.'

'I like it.'

The boy wandered around the house, touching furniture and ornaments, even doors and windows as if seeing them for the first time. Matt grated parmesan over the bowls of steaming pasta and took them to the dining table.

'Dig in.' He speared a tube of rigatoni with his fork. Dylan reached into his bowl with his hand.

'No! You'll burn yourself.'

Matt waved his fork in front of Dylan, indicating the fork beside the boy's napkin. Dylan examined it carefully, then stabbed a piece of pasta and put it in his mouth. He began asking questions. Lots of questions. Did Matt live on the beach? How many other people lived there? What foods did they eat?

What did they do with their time? Did he think all people might live in the sea one day? Some of the questions were so bizarre, Matt thought the boy might really be a bit mad.

'You'd better get some sleep. You can have my bed,' Matt said.

'What about you?'

'I can sleep on the couch.'

'It doesn't look very comfortable.'

'I'll be okay.'

'No, I want you to sleep in the bed too.'

'I shouldn't.'

'Why not?'

Matt couldn't think of a reason. Dylan was beautiful. He wanted to be close to him. 'Well, if you're okay with it?'

'I am.'

They lay down and Matt pulled the covers over them. He felt Dylan take his hand and gently rub his thumb back and forth across his palm. Matt grew hard quickly. He put his arm around Dylan, pulling him closer, kissing his forehead, his cheek, his neck. The boy's lips tasted of the sea. The smell of his skin was like foaming surf. Now Dylan was on top of him, sitting upright, easing back on him, smooth and slippery. His gliding elasticity, like warm bread, sent electrifying pulses through Matt's body. Dylan rested his hands on Matt's shoulders as he took him in deeper. Matt let him lead, and the boy teased him onwards, closer and closer to the moment when everything surged and the world was only a blinding light.

*

When Matt woke up, he found he was hugging Dylan tight. The morning light had painted the room nectarine bright. He left the boy to sleep. From the porch, he watched the sun cast its first diamonds into the sea.

Dylan wanted to swim after breakfast. They walked hand in hand along the beach. The air was hot, the water warm and vivid under a cerulean sky. Dylan stripped naked and waded into the surf, his shins and ankles spattered by the tide's frothy margins. Matt splashed after him, aroused, churning up the salty water as he swam towards the boy. Dylan turned, waving and beckoning. Matt reached out but the boy disappeared underwater, looping around him like a young seal. Matt dived, and opened his eyes as Dylan kissed him. They twisted downwards, deeper and deeper into the soundless underworld. Matt felt the sudden need for air, tensed against the instinct to panic. Dylan pushed his tongue into Matt's mouth, breathing into him, working Matt's hardness with his fingers. Matt felt his passion erupt, spiky white strands suspended in the cooling water.

They swam back to shore and lay together on the sand. The sky was empty. Matt felt the rising breeze, ample and fresh, teasing his skin as he drifted into sleep.

*

Matt sat up, looking up and down the shoreline, scanning the wide, glimmering sea. The sun was high overhead and there was no sign of the boy. He ran into the surf, shouting Dylan's name but the undulating sea gave nothing away. He felt alone and belittled by the sea's absolute indifference. Then something flickered in the distant blue. Before Matt could make out what it was, it vanished again. A few moments later he saw it once more, much closer this time: Dylan was darting through the water at an incredible speed. The boy stood up in the shallows and strode towards the beach.

Matt hugged him and kissed him. 'I thought you'd drowned.'

'Why?'

'I couldn't see you.'

'I was just out there. Just under the water.'

'I thought I'd lost you.'

Dylan took Matt's hand and they wandered slowly back towards the beach house, kicking their feet in the surf.

The house was cool and dark after the glare of the beach. Matt made chicken sandwiches and grabbed two Peronis from the fridge. He switched on the television and soon felt Dylan's head heavy against his shoulder. He guessed the boy wasn't used to alcohol.

*

Dylan ran outside and knelt on the sand, breathing in bellyfuls of fresh air. He felt sick and dizzy and his head ached.

'I shouldn't have given you beer,' Matt said. 'I'm sorry.'

'Does everybody drink beer?'

'Not everybody.'

Matt folded his arms around Dylan. 'You smell so good I could eat you up.'

'Matt, let's go back for one last swim before it gets dark.'

They raced each other to the sea.

Rain clouds had gathered to the east and the temperature had dipped, the waves were rolling more forcefully into shore. Dylan was ahead, powering out into the greying expanse. Matt's arms struck the water, legs whipping up foam behind him. He had to keep stopping to make sure he didn't lose sight of the boy. He turned back towards the beach and saw they were a long way from land now. Matt was a little afraid of the sea's wide plain but also intoxicated by its terrible beauty. Dylan came to him.

'Stay close,' Matt said. 'I don't want to lose you.'

'Do you love me?' Dylan asked him, dark eyes blazing.

'Yes.'

'I need something from you.'

'Anything.'

'I need you to give me your soul. Without it, I'll cease to exist. I'll vanish into the sea forever. Will you do it? Will you give me your soul?'

Matt looked towards the beach. The sun had dipped below the horizon. The land was no more than a thin dark strip against the dusky sky. He took hold of the boy, savouring him. His tangle of wet hair, his long lashes, the cool magenta of his lips.

'Yes,' he whispered. 'I'll give you my soul,'

Dylan kissed him, holding him tight, dragging him quickly down beneath the surface. Deeper and deeper, fathoms deep. Matt's senses gave out as the brutal darkness took him.

*

For a long time, the sea was empty. The only sound was the soulful murmuring of the waves. Then the calm was broken as the boy somersaulted high out of the water, now slicing back through the surface in an acrobatic downward arc. He came up again, body twisting in the moonlight, his face bright but forlorn. He started to swim purposefully towards the shore.

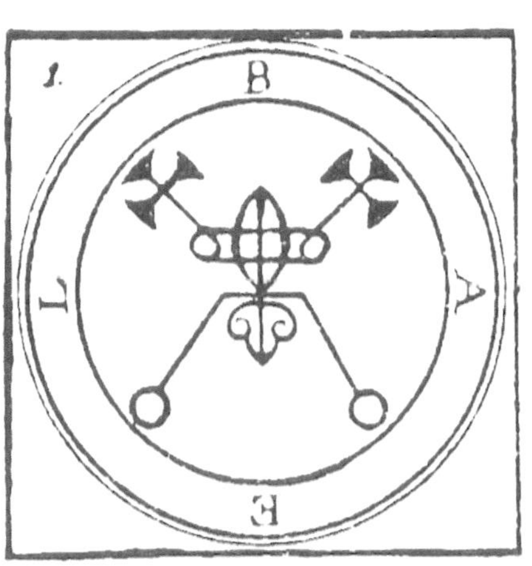

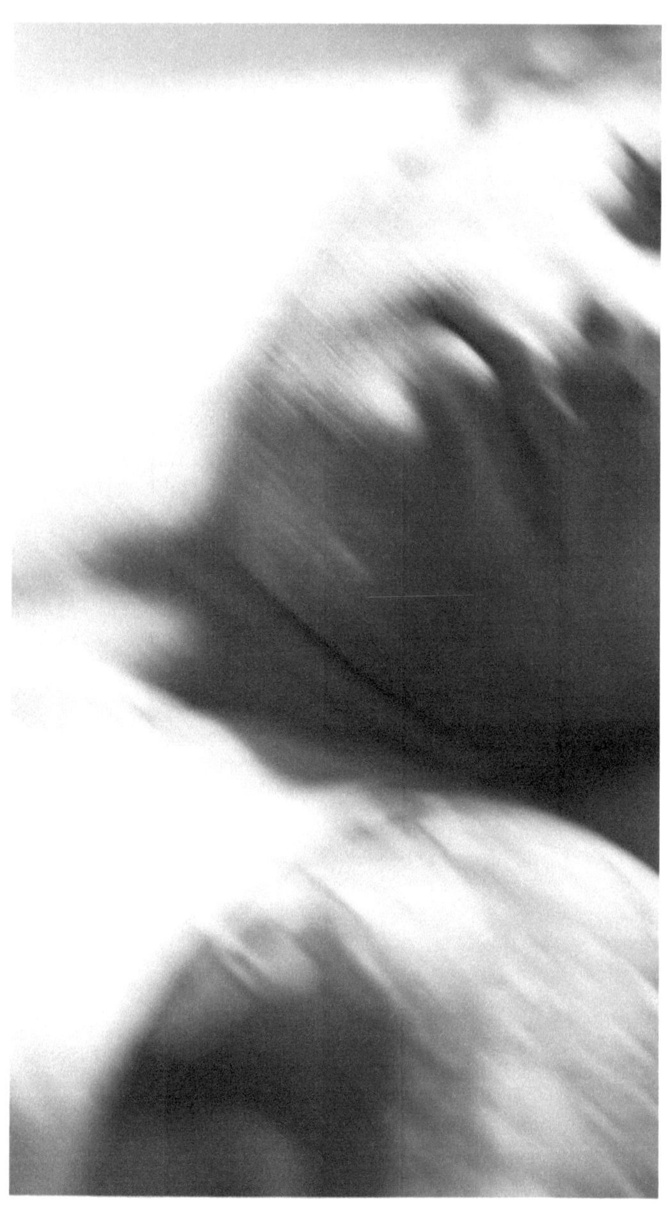

'Clem was lying on the bed.
He seemed restless.'

CLEM

I looked around at my little kitchen garden. The breeze was getting cooler every day now. I picked up a couple more potatoes and threw them into the basket, then turned to check the old mill. Everything was quiet. I walked back past raised beds of colourful squash and sweetcorn, ready for harvesting. Gravel scraped and crunched underfoot. The mill had been converted about five years ago. It made a large and comfortable house, plenty of room for Clem and me. I decided to check on him. I left the basket by the step and went upstairs. I knocked gently on Clem's door and went in.

Clem was lying on the bed. He seemed restless. I pulled up a chair and sat by him. 'Take it easy sweetheart. No need to be so on edge. It's almost lunchtime. I'm going to make myself a lovely leek and potato soup. It's a shame you don't like it.'

His eyes were watery, his condition was getting worse. I wasn't sure if he knew what I was saying but it didn't really matter. Being here together was what counted. I took his hand gently in mine. He tried to raise himself up off the bed. I stood up. His lips moved. Was he trying to say my name?

'That's it, darling, say it: Michael.'

No sound came.

'Just lie still and rest. I'll be back in a little while.'

I blew him a kiss and closed the door behind me.

*

I peeled the potatoes, and sliced leeks and onions for the soup. Once everything was simmering, I found my special spot in the sitting room. The previous owners had kept the mill's mechanism intact. Through a small glass panel you could watch the water cascading from the mill stream. I sat down and began my daily meditation. I let my gaze soften and rest on the soapy foam of the rushing water. Some days it was harder than others to settle in the present moment. This was one of those days. After a couple of minutes, I gave up and went back into the kitchen. I buttered slices of bread and checked the pan. When the vegetables were tender, I pureed the soup mixture and left it bubbling on the hot plate.

I took Clem something to eat and he seemed to brighten up a little. Then I came back downstairs and ate my lunch alone in the dining room. After the washing up, I stretched out on the sofa with the last chapter of a John Fowles novel.

*

The sudden shattering sound of glass in the kitchen. Next, the click of the latch on the back door. I picked up the fire poker. Careful footsteps. Then a dishevelled-looking kid crept into the sitting room. I raised the poker above my head and leapt at him.

'Terry, look out!' I hadn't reckoned on the girl coming in behind. I hesitated, and the kid slammed his fist into my face. The next thing I knew, I was on the floor. There was a buzzing in my head and the boy was on top of me, pinning my arms down with his knees, his crotch in my face.

'Careful Terry! He looks like a loony.'

'Shut up, Sonia.'

Their faces were dirty. Terry's bomber jacket was ripped along one sleeve and there was blood on his tee shirt. He twisted my chin, grinding my cheek into the floor. 'The nice man's going to do just what we tell him.'

I nodded.

'Good boy.'

He climbed off me, reached in his jacket pocket and pulled out a kitchen knife. 'I picked this up on my way in.'

I pushed myself up onto my elbows. 'What do you want?'

'How about everything you've got, mate?' Terry balled his fist round my collar and dragged me to my feet.

'What's in here?' Sonia pointed to the storeroom.

'Nothing.' Something told them I was lying.

'Why don't we all take a look?' Terry shoved me forward.

As we walked past the stairs, I prayed Clem would keep quiet.

'No funny business.' Terry pressed the knife into my ribs as we went into the storeroom. Sonia pushed past us and stopped dead.

'Bloody hell,' she said.

Terry stared in disbelief then asked, mocking me, 'What's all this?'

In the corner of the room was my altar to Clem. It was covered by a large black cloth. In the centre stood a burning pillar candle and a shirtless photo of Clem in a gilt frame. Around these were scattered several faded rose petals, locks of his hair, a pair of his briefs and other mementoes from before.

Terry stepped closer to me, his face inches from mine. 'Who's this bloke? Your bum chum?'

Sonia giggled.

'Who's a pervy little Buttercup, then?' Terry shoved me hard and I slammed into the altar, knocking Clem's picture to the floor. Terry crushed the glass under the heel of his boot, pulled Clem's crumpled photo out of the wreckage and dangled it in my face.

'Don't, Terry.' Sonia stood a few feet away, arms folded, staring nervously at the floor. I wondered how many times she'd felt the back of Terry's hand. He glanced at her, then let the photo fall. I watched it float gently to the ground. Terry thrust the kitchen knife under my chin. 'I'm hungry,' he said. 'Come on, Buttercup. Why don't you be a good little girlie and make me a nice sandwich? Then we can decide what to do with you.'

'I'm not going to fight you,' I said.

'You wouldn't stand a chance.'

*

'How would you like your sandwich?'

'Ham and pickle, and a packet of crisps… please, Buttercup.' He grinned and sat down on one of the kitchen stools.

'The ham's run out. But there's tinned tuna?'

'All right.'

'There isn't any butter either.'

'Fine. Just get on with it.' He began drumming his fingers on the table. I took a tin of tuna from the cupboard and reached for the loaf of bread.

'I'm going to need a knife to cut the bread.'

'Get one out of the drawer. Slowly.' He stood up and watched as I picked out a long, serrated bread knife. 'Not that one, clever Dick. Drop it back inside.' He motioned me to stand back then pulled out a small butter knife.

'I can't cut with that.'

'You'll cut with it or I'll cut you.'

A stuttering scream from upstairs. I realised Sonia was no longer in the room with us. Terry bundled me out of the kitchen. Sonia appeared, running down the stairs, stumbling over the last few steps.

'What the fuck's the matter with you?' For the first time, I heard uncertainty in Terry's voice.

'Oh, my God.' Sonia staggered to her feet. She pointed up at the gallery. 'He's got one of them up in his room. He's got a fucking zombie in there!'

Terry rounded on me. 'You're keeping one as a pet?'

I didn't know how to answer him. He wouldn't understand.

He turned to Sonia, 'Show me.'

'I don't want to go up there again.'

He moved towards her and she flinched. 'Show me! Buttercup can lead the way.'

Clem's door was half open. I pushed it wide. Clem was hanging off the side of the bed. I had tied his wrists to the bedstead but the ropes were frayed where he had gnawed at them. Scattered around the room were discarded bones. Human. Terry nudged past me into the room.

'Oh, Jesus Christ.'

Clem twisted, tugging at his restraints.

'It's that bloke in the picture downstairs,' Sonia said. 'Kill it, Terry! Kill it!'

I couldn't let them hurt Clem. I ran at Terry, beating him back with my fists. He dropped the knife and stumbled. Clem lunged, his teeth sinking into the boy's shoulder. Terry thrashed wildly. Sonia screamed and backed away. The ropes holding Clem tore apart. Now Terry started yelling, dragging himself across the floor as Clem bit into his shoulder again and again. Sonia turned to run. I stuck my foot out to trip her up, yanked the bedside lamp out of its socket, and hit her with it hard. I threw the lamp into the hallway, hauled Sonia out of the room and slammed the door shut. I hit her again and again and again with the base of the lamp until I was certain she was dead, then carried her body downstairs. No need to worry about Clem for the moment. He would be calm for a while. He always was after feeding.

I took Sonia's corpse into the storeroom and laid it on the floor. I found my saw and set to work. It was dark outside by the time I had finished. I removed the covering from Clem's altar and opened the lid of the large chest freezer underneath. The reassuring hum reminded me how lucky Clem and I were that the mill still had a working generator. The mill's previous owners, filleted and jointed, were piled up inside, but there was still room for Sonia. A welcome addition to Clem's larder. I loved Clem. I would always love him. All I needed was to keep him safely tucked away. I collected some rope from the shed then went up to his room. I pushed open the door. I could see him standing in the shadows.

'Clem, it's me. They're gone now. No need to worry. It's just us, just you and me.'

I stepped into the room. He began to move towards me in the dark.

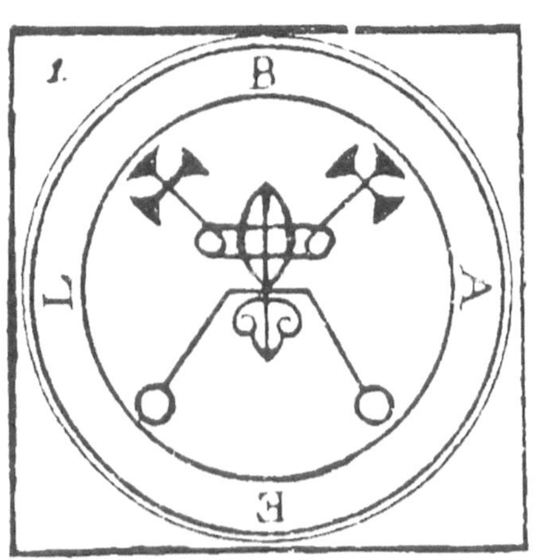

*'Finn ran her fingers
through Macy's soft curls.'*

CHILDREN OF SIRIUS

The earth is a petri dish, an experiment instigated by the Great Beings from the galaxy of Sirius. The purest of the human race will be saved from the earth's destruction. Those chosen few are the Children of Sirius. At solstice in the 21st year of the 21st century, the Children of Sirius will ascend. On the Day of the Ascension the Great Beings will take the earthly Children aboard their vessel, and transport them to a new home in a distant galaxy. Only the Child's consciousness will be teleported. To ascend, each Child must leave the physical body behind, in death. FROM THE BOOK OF THE ASCENSION, THIRD BOOK OF SIRIUS.

For seven years, Finn had devoted her life to the Children of Sirius. She had worked hard, spreading the colony's message of salvation, ever since they had taken over an abandoned nuclear bunker on Greensea Island. Now *The Children* numbered more than a hundred. People on the mainland called them a cult. But they saw themselves as *the chosen few*. Finn used to believe that. Now her faith was gone. Now she was running.

She slipped out of the dormitory as soon as the others were asleep. The lights in the corridor flickered and hummed. Shadows leapt and shrank. No one was allowed outside the dorms after midnight. Anyone breaking the rules was punished. She had arranged to meet Macy in front of the refectory but there was no sign of her. Macy's dormitory was on the farthest side of the bunker. What if one of the brethren had intercepted her? Finn pressed herself against the wall at the sound of approaching footsteps. Seconds later, Macy appeared. Finn hugged her, kissed her, ran her fingers through Macy's soft curls, smelled her soft dark skin. 'I thought you weren't coming!'

'I had to wait a little longer. Not everyone went to sleep straight away.'

Finn took the lead, pausing at the compound's exit. At least one of the brethren would be on watch.

'Remember what we talked about, Macy. Can you do it?'

'I think so.'

Macy disappeared outside. Finn listened.

'Jesus, Macy! You scared the shit out of me. What the hell are you doing out here?' The voice belonged to Paulus, one of the younger colony members.

'I couldn't sleep. I needed some air.'

'You'd better get back inside. You know the penalty for breaking curfew.'

'I don't care.'

'But they'll flay you!'

'They'll have to catch me first.'

'What's got into you, Macy?'

'I don't know. It's Ascension Day.'

'Are you scared?' asked Paulus.

'Aren't you?'

Finn landed her punch. The impact snapped his head sideways and he crumpled to the ground. Finn bent over him, gently tapping his face.

'He's out cold.'

'Is he going to be okay? You hit him pretty hard.'

'He'll be fine. But he'll have the mother of all hangovers when he wakes up.'

They left the compound quickly and headed up the track through the brush. The colony's dock lay about two miles north. The brethren used it to moor their fishing boats, and to land supplies from the mainland. Finn planned to steal a boat and get off the island for good. The last place she wanted to be was on Greensea Island at sunset tomorrow when the brethren gathered in the bunker's dining hall, when dusk came, when each took the required dose of cyanide to end their lives.

Clouds drifted across the moon. Finn flicked on her torch and the beam sliced through the darkness.

'You're very quiet, Macy.'

'We are doing the right thing, aren't we?'

'Yes.'

'But what if there really is a new world, and a better life?'

'There isn't.'

'You used to be so certain.'

'We aren't the chosen ones. There are no Great Beings.'

'You can't know that for sure.'

'Look at us, Macy. Look at what we've become. The colony was supposed to be about peace and brotherhood and community while we waited for Ascension. Now we have curfews, and beatings for people who don't follow the rules.'

'But we're only human. When we ascend, it'll be different.'

'Nobody's going to ascend. At sunset tomorrow, all those people in the bunker are going to die. We need to get off this island and tell the police.'

'You want to stop Ascension?'

'We can't just run away and do nothing. We'd have their blood on our hands.'

'You used to have the strongest faith of all of us, Finn.'

'I woke up.'

The sound of voices floated out of the darkness. Finn killed the torch and they ducked into the undergrowth. Torchlight swung and zigzagged as two men passed close by, heading in the direction of the bunker.

'That was Josh and Eric,' Finn said. 'What are they doing out after curfew?'

'Maybe the Council of Elders decided to run some patrols.'

'I didn't know anything about that.'

'Perhaps they want to make sure no one turns up from the mainland so close to Ascension.'

'We'd better go across the scrub. It'll slow us down but at least it'll give us some cover.'

'When Josh and Eric get back to the compound, they'll find Paulus.'

Finn frowned. They'd raise the alarm and the brethren would come hunting for them.

Finn was wondering if walking through the scrub had been the best idea after all when something moved in the undergrowth close to Macy. Macy gasped sharply and crumpled. Finn reached her just in time to see the adder's grey back disappear into the undergrowth. She unfastened Macy's sandal. The skin was already swelling around two livid puncture marks. Macy was breathing erratically. Finn cupped her face in her hands. 'Look at me, Macy.'

'What was that?'

'An adder.'

'Am I going to die?'

'No, you're not.'

Finn tried to sound reassuring. 'You'll need an anti-venom, that's all. We have to go to a hospital.

Can you walk?'

'I think so.'

*

Macy leaned heavily on Finn's shoulder. Finn could just make out the brethren's fishing hut on the grassy rise before the long slope of the beach. The hut was always left unlocked. She foraged inside for the first aid kit and set to work, cleaning and bandaging Macy's ankle. She gave Macy two painkillers.

'I feel really sick, Finn.'

'You're going to be okay. I promise.'

Voices sounded again in the distance. Finn and Macy flattened themselves in the scrub. The brethren had started their search. 'Still no sign of them.'

'Maybe they're hiding out and we've already passed them.'

'Search from here to the sea then double back.'

Two of the brethren set off towards the beach. A third checked the hut then stood at the edge of the path, training his torch over the open scrubland. After a while, all three men hurried back in the direction of the bunker, and were swallowed up by the night.

'I think I'm going to throw up.' Macy turned away and wretched.

'That's a normal reaction to the venom.'

'I feel so dizzy.'

'You're going to be all right. We're going to get off this island and to a doctor.'

Finn lifted Macy in her arms and carried her towards the beach. From the crest of the rise, Finn saw waves tumbling in to shore. White foam sloshed at the feet of the long timber jetty. Two small rowing boats bobbed and tugged against their moorings. Finn stumbled down the grassy incline and onto the sand. She lay Macy down beside the jetty and went to check the boats. One was waterlogged but the other one was dry. The mainland was a mile away, give or take. She would need all her strength to row against the tide. She carried Macy to the boat. Macy's eyes were closed. She was breathing heavily. Her face was ash-pale.

Finn pushed the boat out into the ink-black water. The lights of the mainland looked very far away. She fought with the oars as waves beat the boat back towards shore. Then the brethren re-appeared, sprinting along the beach, training torches onto the waves, running into the surf, swimming out towards them. Finn rowed hard but one of the brethren grabbed the side of the boat. Finn pulled an oar from its rowlock and swung it down hard on his shoulder. He disappeared under the water, then surfaced, rocking the hull, trying to tip Finn out. She pitched forwards onto the wooden planking, losing the oar over the side. All three of the brethren were at the boat now. Finn realised she couldn't make the crossing, or risk a fight - if the boat capsized Macy would drown.

*

As they lifted Macy back onto the dock, Finn said quietly, 'She's been bitten by an adder. She needs a doctor.'

One of the brethren examined her. 'She won't be needing any doctors where she's going.'

'She could die before Ascension. Do you want that on your conscience?'

He paused for a moment then nodded to his companions. 'Take her over to the mainland. Dump her on the beach. Someone will find her soon enough.'

'Someone should stay with her,' said Finn. 'Please, just let us both go. We don't belong here anymore.'

He took a step closer and grabbed Finn by both arms. 'What do you mean, Finn? Of course you belong here. You're our leader.'

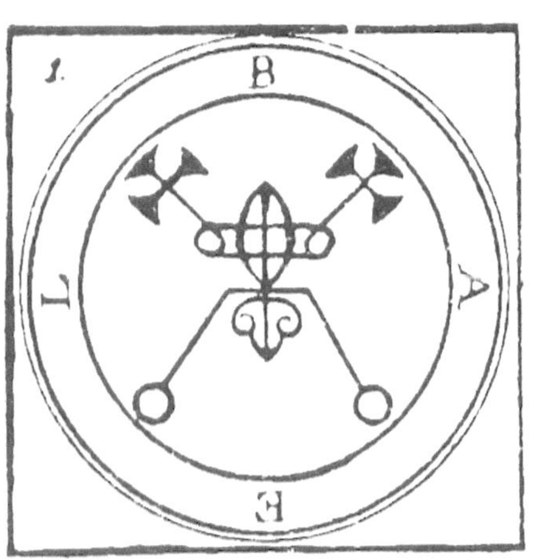

*'Our bodies stirred
as they touched.'*

FORBIDDEN

4TH DECEMBER 1957

A Vauxhall Cresta crawls along a greying country road. On either side, freezing fog forms a dank stain, obscuring the Fenlands like so much dirty cotton wool. It will be sundown in under an hour. The two men in the Vauxhall are lost.

I traced my finger along the map - the turning should be just ahead. Doug was leaning over the steering wheel nervously like an expectant father. I squeezed his thigh and he gave me a milky smile. A bend in the lane offered us a by-road along a narrow spinney.

'Shall we try this?' Doug asked.

'What have we got to lose? Don't you remember the place at all?'

'The last time I was here, I was ten. I'm as much in the dark as you are.'

The fog swallowed up the road. Doug changed down to second, and edged along the uneven track.

The Cresta rocks drunkenly from side to side. Its headlights pick out a narrow stone bridge. Doug guides the car tentatively between mossy balustrades to avoid scraping the paintwork. Beyond a dark line of oaks, the road opens out in front of an impressive front-gabled Victorian mansion.

Doug leaned over and kissed me, like a man who had been given a last-minute reprieve. 'We made it, Frank.'

'Just.'

I looked up at the apex of the slate roof, stark and black against the dirty fog. 'So this is uncle's house?'

'Yes,' Doug said. 'The puritanical old goat. I remember childhood summers here, bored to death, listening to his sermons.'

'You shouldn't speak ill of the dead.'

'That's what they say. Let's take a look inside.'

The entrance hall is painted a cloudy grey-green and smells of mildew. In the drawing room, gilded candelabras stand on top of a commanding fireplace. There is a worn Chesterfield sofa and, opposite, two red

I rested a hand on Doug's shoulder. 'So, how does it feel to be the new lord of the manor?'

'A bit strange, I suppose. I wouldn't want to live here full time. But it might be an inspiring place for you to work for a while. Just the kind of place Madame Blavatsky would have hung out in.'

'True.'

'A few days here and you'll easily finish the last chapter.'

'Are you chivvying me along in your capacity as my editor or my illicit lover?'

'Both.'

Doug turned me towards him and I lifted my head to meet his lips. Our bodies stirred as they touched, hungry for what was forbidden. I pulled away, mindful of the large bay window behind us. What if someone was watching the house? 'There are a couple of valises in the boot that need rescuing, handsome.'

'Sure,' Doug said. 'How about I do that and you see if you can rustle up some tea?'

I closed the curtains against the advancing darkness. The kitchen was high-ceilinged, airy and bare compared with the rest of the house. I found an old copper kettle and lit the burner. Doug's uncle had died less than a month ago - I reckoned the tea in the caddy would still be reasonably fresh.

I heard Doug's heavy footfalls on the stairs and found him up in the master bedroom. The fourposter bed had been made up neatly.

'Looks like someone's got the place ready for us,' I said.

'Uncle Nathaniel's housekeeper.'

I raised my eyebrows.

'Don't worry,' Doug said. 'She doesn't live in. But, speaking of which.'

He took my suitcase and put it in the other bedroom.

'Just in case she pops round unannounced.'

There were two studies, one upstairs, one on the ground floor. The only typewriter in the house was a clunky old Royal Signet with no shift key. I realised I was going to have to write the last chapter longhand. The housekeeper had left a chicken pie in the kitchen for us, and we ate it hungrily, listening to the radio. The lead story was the London rail disaster. At St. John's Railway Station, just outside Lewisham, two trains had collided in heavy fog when one of the drivers missed the stop signal. As one train veered into a bridge, it collapsed onto carriages packed with rush hour commuters below. The other main story was the first parliamentary debate on the Wolfenden Report, instigated by Lord Pakenham.

'Do you think they'll ever decriminalise?' I asked.

Doug shrugged. 'If they do, it won't be for years

yet, specially with Kilmuir as Lord High Chancellor. He's got too much power. In Great Britain we prefer leisurely revolutions.'

'This would be one hell of a revolution.'

'You and I, my darling, are going to have to continue operating undercover for the foreseeable future.' He squeezed my hand but I didn't return his smile.

'You make it sound so glamorous but we're really just skulking about in the shadows.'

'Come on, it's not so bad. We've got chicken pie.'

Doug always knew how to buoy me up.

'But nothing to drink.'

'Uncle Nathaniel was a teetotal sourpuss. We could buy some tomorrow, maybe pop into Cambridge? In the meantime, I'm sure we can entertain ourselves without wine.' Doug stood up, extended his hand. 'Shall we retire to the bedroom, beautiful?'

It took Doug a long time to get the fire going. We huddled together under the icy sheets, pressing close for warmth. It had been a while since we'd been alone like this and I nestled into Doug eagerly. The swirling hairs on his chest tickled my face as I traced my hand across his stomach. He swiped a drop of vaseline onto his fingers and readied me. Then he forged inside, his movements strong and measured, resisting the urge to climax too soon. His hands gripped mine, knuckles white, and I kissed his lips as his fire flowed through me. He stayed inside as long as he could, resting his head next to mine, and we sailed away into sleep.

*

I woke up needing a pee. The bedside clock said 2am. Doug had shifted away from me, turning on his side to face the window. His breathing was slow and heavy. The fire had long since died and the room was very cold. I crossed the landing to the bathroom, lifted the toilet seat, steadied my aim, and leaned forward to gaze out the window. There was someone standing outside in the dark, staring back up at me. I skidded backwards on the tiles and cracked the back of my head on the sink as I went down. The next thing I knew, Doug was crouching beside me and I was watching multi-coloured blotches flare and fade behind my eyes.

Doug walked me across the hall. I sat on the edge of the bed and he examined the bump on my head. 'What happened?'

'I saw someone. There was a man outside looking up. It startled me and I must have slipped.'

Doug went over to the window. 'There's nobody there now.'.

'There was someone, Doug.'

'I think you're very tired. You were probably half asleep, still dreaming perhaps, spooked yourself in a strange house.'

'No, there was someone out there.'

'Shhh,' he whispered and pulled me close.

Doug was a very rational, practical man. I knew he didn't believe me. Back in bed, I lay on my side, trying to get comfortable. Why would someone be standing outside the house, in the freezing cold, at two in the morning? I shut my eyes. My head was throbbing, then the walls of the mansion were pressing in blackly around me.

*

The fog had almost disappeared and the morning sun was starting to burn through the haze. Doug insisted on calling the local physician, a well-fed, squire-of-the-manor type, businesslike with a bullish tone. He diagnosed a 'nasty old bump' but no concussion, instructing me to take Fizrin Instant Seltzers at regular intervals and avoid exertion. Then he trotted back to his cherry red AC Ace and sped away, churning up a little mud in his wake. We abandoned our trip into Cambridge, and Doug spent the rest of the day poring over manuscripts. I made painfully slow work on my biography, researching A.P. Sinnett's *Incidents in the Life of Madame Blavatsky*. In the evening we listened to the radio again and finished the rest of the chicken pie. Harold Watkinson, Minister of Transport and Civil Aviation, announced an inquiry into the rail disaster and paid tribute to the work of the emergency services. The death toll now stood at seventy-six.

*

Doug was already asleep. I lay next to him in the suffocating darkness. When I finally drifted off, my dreams were full of wolves, fitful shadows, minacious wolf howls, shapes in the dark. By 2am I needed another Instant Seltzer, and was craving a cup of tea. I got up as quietly as possible to avoid waking Doug.

I was grateful for the moonlight, bright through the tall arches of the windows in the kitchen. I put the kettle on, dropped an Instant Seltzer into a glass of water, and sat down at the table. A face appeared briefly at the window obscured by some kind of black cowl. I dropped my water glass. The glass broke on the floor and I ran headlong into Doug as I raced back up the stairs.

'What's going on, darling? What was all that noise?'

'There's someone outside again. Outside the kitchen window.'

'You stay here. I'll take a look.'

'Careful, there's broken glass on the kitchen floor. I'll come too.'

The kettle was whistling angrily. Doug switched off the gas.

'You saw someone through this window?'

I nodded.

'Okay. I'll go and look around.'

Cold flooded the kitchen as Doug unbolted the back door and went out into the night. The trees hissed like geese in the wind. The door creaked on its hinges and I reached out with tented fingers to steady it.

'Doug?'

No answer. The tops of the oaks were whipping backwards and forwards. The moon rode dark waves of racing clouds. A shadow fell suddenly across the step and I was ready to slam the door in the face of the assailant.

But Doug appeared instead.

'There's no one out there. I've been around the whole house.'

'I definitely did see someone.'

'It'll all look different in the morning. Let's clear up the broken glass and get back to sleep.'

*

The next day we slept in, then Doug drove us to Cambridge. We bought a couple of dinner suits at Eaden Lilley followed by two lacklustre fish salads at the Lyons' Corner House.

'How are you feeling today?' Doug was stacking tomatoes and lettuce onto his fork.

'My headache's gone.'

'And no more visions of men lurking in the bushes?'

'I really did see someone, Doug.'

'Your imagination can play tricks, especially in a strange house, in the dark.'

'What if there's a local Satanic cult and they just don't like strangers?'

'What if aliens have landed in the woods?' Doug laughed.

We got back at sundown. The shadows of the oaks were long against the front of the house. Doug unloaded the car, and I broke open the bottle of Mouquin we'd picked up in Cambridge. We settled in front of the fire and Doug told me about his plans to sell the house. I was relieved. I'd been afraid he might want to use it as a second home or secret love nest. I was starting to feel the mellowing effects of the brandy. Doug unbuttoned my shirt and ran his fingers through the patch of hair between my chest and navel. I unzipped him and he fluttered and grew in my hand. I covered his firmness with my mouth. Suddenly there was a heavy pounding at the front door. Doug zipped himself up clumsily and went over to the window. 'I can't see who it is,' he said. 'They're standing inside the porch.'

The knocking came again.

I followed Doug into the hallway. He started to open the door but was thrown against the wall as the door was forced open from the other side.

A hooded figure enters. He is tall and powerful, with a pronounced chin and nose. A prominent brow juts over deeply-set eyes. A butcher's knife glints in the light as he strikes out at Doug, hacking at his hands and arms.

I ran at the intruder, aiming my knee sharply into his groin. He fell back. The force of his falling body slammed the door shut, locking him in with us. I tried to drag Doug away. Doug's blood was snaking in a slow trail across the floor. The man leapt at me, riding me backwards. We spun across the floor in a macabre embrace as he slashed at me with the knife. I felt a burning sensation in my chest and saw a dark patch spreading across my shirt. I kicked and punched wildly to stop the blade striking home a second time. I landed a glancing blow to his temple and he staggered sideways. I clambered up the stairs. His breathing was close behind. His arm caught around my neck as we came up onto the landing. The blade glinted and arced towards me, and I thrust my elbows into his stomach as hard as I could. Stairs, walls and ceiling revolved in a sudden blur. Then I was lying at the bottom of the staircase. The intruder was lying underneath me, unmoving. Warily, I turned him over. His eyes told me he was dead. Doug was shaking and drenched with sweat. My own injuries were superficial compared to his. I bandaged his arms with towels as best I could then phoned for an ambulance, and then the police.

Doug had lost a lot of blood but the ambulance men said he was going to be okay. When the police arrived, they recognised the attacker: Seth Burke, the estate gardener. Like Doug's uncle, he was a puritan, a firm believer in hellfire and damnation. When the police searched his body, they found a small pocket diary with his pledge to watch over the house, ensuring it remained a place of 'good morals'.

An Inspector Ronald Weston took charge of the crime scene.

'Mr. Burke believed he was doing the Lord's work,' the balding Inspector told me. 'He believed you and Douglas Henstridge were deviants. Do you have any idea why he might have formed that impression, sir?'

'No, Inspector, I don't.'

'Why were you and Mr. Henstridge in the house?'

'Doug inherited it when his uncle died. He wanted to check it over before putting it up for sale.'

'And why did he need you here, Mr. Blakeley?'

'He's my editor and I needed somewhere peaceful to finish my book.'

'What is your book about, if you don't mind my asking?'

'Not at all, Inspector. It's about Madame Blavatsky.'

'Madame Blavatsky?'

'The founder of the Theosophical Society.'

'I'm not familiar with it.'

'It's a spiritual organisation.'

'Christian?'

'No.'

'I see.'

A uniformed police officer enters the room. He glances at Frank Blakeley oddly for a moment then mutters something conspiratorially in the Inspector's ear.

'Inspector, when can I go and see Doug?' I asked.

'Hold on a minute, sir. We're not quite finished yet.' He took a deep breath and looked around the room before returning his gaze to me. 'How long have you been staying here with Mr. Henstridge?'

'Since Wednesday.'

'So, two nights?'

'Yes. Two nights.'

'It appears that only one bed has been slept in during those two nights. The one in the master bedroom. There's a suitcase in the second bedroom, but the bed is undisturbed.'

I had no idea what to say.

'Sodomy is a criminal offence in the United Kingdom, Mr. Blakeley. Have you engaged in sexual perversion with Mr. Henstridge? Are you a pervert, a homosexual?'

'Danny was wearing only a clinging tee shirt,
Levis and Caterpillar boots.'

45 MINUTES

Pete took a drag on his cigarette and checked the clock on the wall again. Forty-five minutes till midnight. 'It only ever happens after midnight,' was one of the first things Benny had told him.

Benny had been unemployed and sofa-surfing. Then he acquired an ugly little fetish-doll from the Caribbean and, in just a few months, he had a seven-figure income, homes in Antigua and the Hamptons, and a dozen vintage sports cars divided between the two.

Then there were the women. Benny was always talking about the women.

Benny was one of those guys who just drifted through life. In the end, he gave the fetish-doll to Pete, and Pete knew exactly what he wanted from it.

For years Pete had struggled to make a mark in the record industry. Now he was offered a job producing a promising young band. The first album rocketed to the top of the Billboard charts and stayed there for ten weeks. After that, Pete's future was secure. He had the magic touch. He became the go-to guy for some of the greatest names in rock. He worked at Abbey Road, Capitol Studios, Sound City, Question de Son, never staying in one place for more than a few months. That's how he managed to stay one step ahead of the doll's darker side. But each time he moved on, he had the sense that the end was getting closer.

Pete had spent seven nomadic years looking over his shoulder. Now he was burned out. It was time to man-up and face his fate. He could have passed the fetish on, of course, but its hold on him was too strong. Tonight the curse would catch up with him. He was going to die and then the doll's power to harm would die with him.

But he had to admit that the last seven years had been a blast: recording projects in Paris, New York, Berlin, all-night parties high on ecstasy, acid and poppers, any sexual partner, or number of partners, he wanted. He was known across the world as one of the greatest record producers of all time. He guested on *Oprah* and *The Late Show*. Publishers on both sides of the Atlantic competed for the rights to publish his story. But the presidential suite at the Royal Hawaiian or a luxury plantation house in the

Caribbean started to blur into one another. Pete realised he was just tired, tired of running, tired of second-guessing, tired of trying to keep himself out of demonic reach. The horrible clay fetish was toxic with the accumulated corruption and depravity of all its previous owners. That toxin took its toll physically. Horrific migraines floored Pete suddenly with the force of a Sugar Ray Leonard right hook. He suffered from double vision and nauseating dizziness. Benny had gone through something similar towards the end. Benny's headaches got so bad he had to be hospitalised but the doctors could never determine the cause.

So Benny had passed on the pleasure and the pain. He had let Pete have it, in every sense. And that's what did for Benny. Benny's stock market speculations backfired. He lost everything. With his last few hundred pounds, he bought himself a bottle of whisky and a gun, rented a room in a sordid Soho hotel, and ended it.

Pete knew his own life would fall apart just as rapidly if he gave the fetish-doll away. It had a livid, lupine face, and its flesh-coloured clay was forever cold to the touch. Pete asked occult booksellers Treadwell's and Anderson Butler to help him research its origins. Now he owned a stack of obscure volumes and had managed to piece together the doll's fantastical narrative.

The Rite of Marchosias called for an effigy to be made of clay mixed with the blood of an innocent.

The livid mud was to be formed into the likeness of Marchosias, a wolf-demon from the *Ars Goetia*, the first book of the *Lesser Key of Solomon*. After seven rounds of unholy incantations, repeated seven times, the ritual was complete. From that moment, all the necromancer's vices were absorbed by the fetish. His life became enchanted. He rode on a wave of opulence and indulgence. He became invincible. But the cosmos always seeks balance, and a bargain with a devil as powerful as Marchosias comes with a terrible price tag. According to legend, six hundred and sixty-six days after completion of the ritual, a demon from Marchosias's thirty legions will climb out of the pits of hell, searching for the fetish and its owner. Eventually, it will drag them both back down into the abyss. Tonight, this diabolic legacy would end with Pete.

Pete accepted a job in London, producing the world's most successful heavy metal band, Dawn of the Dead. He indulged in a few drug and alcohol-fuelled binges with the group's lead singer, Michael Strang. They went to bed a couple of times but it was nothing spectacular. Pete was just going through the motions. He had already engaged in almost every sexual act known to man. Sex simply didn't do anything for him anymore.

Now he felt somehow relieved as he sat in somebody else's living room, surrounded by somebody else's furniture and somebody's else's possessions. He had rented the cottage because it was well out of the city. This time there would be no more running. If he weakened and called out for help, nobody would hear him. All he hoped for now was a swift end.

He poured himself a generous measure of Glenmorangie and gulped half of it down. The alcohol scorched the back of his throat. He topped up his glass and stepped outside. The garden gave on to gloomy woodland. Spindly trees swayed dimly in the black beyond the lawn. There was no moon and little light from the cottage windows. He shivered, took another swig for courage and went back inside. Pete had encountered the demon once before. It had been sudden, and brutal. But he had survived.

The Burning Trees were on the verge of breaking up. Creative differences between the band members made the sessions extremely difficult. There were frequent stormings-out and they had to be cajoled into returning to work. The recording at Space Mountain Studios was falling further and further behind schedule. The Spanish summer was beautiful but, as the weeks passed, Pete felt a familiar tightening in the pit of his stomach: he had stayed in one place for too long.

There was no air in the villa he had taken for the duration. The evening was hot and still. He fixed himself a coffee and tried to relax. He stretched out on the couch with a magazine. Even after sunset, there'd been no blessed coolness but now, suddenly, the temperature plummeted. Outside, the decking creaked under the weight of something immensely heavy. Pete flicked off the lamp and lay still in the dark. A large shadow moved very swiftly outside the windows towards the front of the villa.

Pete reached the hallway just as the beating started on the front door. His car keys were on the nightstand in the bedroom. If he could make it to the Porsche, he could probably outrun Marchosias's demon. He sprinted into the bedroom, plucked up the keys, rifled through his bedside drawers looking for the fetish. Then he heard the front door break open explosively. He jumped out of the bedroom window, and landed awkwardly. Pain shot up through his left shoulder. He could hear the cursed thing moving inside the villa, crashing from room to room.

Searching.

He made a run for it, jabbing at the key fob until the locks on the Porsche snapped open. He threw the fetish onto the passenger seat and forced himself to guide the car key slowly and methodically into the ignition, only managing to press it home on the third attempt because his hands were trembling so violently. The engine screamed into life. Something thudded heavily against the side of the car. He stamped on the accelerator. Tyres whirled on gravel. Dust spewed into the air. The car lurched forward and careened down the driveway. Pete glimpsed the massive bulk of Marchosias's demon rebounding from the impact with the car. Then Pete was gripping the steering wheel for dear life, and the car was spinning out onto the road, and missing a tree by inches, and the demonic cry was retreating behind him as he sped away into the night.

A knocking at the door startled him out of his reverie. His hand slipped and he spilled whisky on the rug. He was aware suddenly of his own heartbeat. Was it time already? The knocking came again and this time he recognised the sharp rat-a-tat of a human hand. Danny Alexander, his trainee sound engineer, stood shivering in the doorway. Danny was wearing only a clinging tee shirt, Levis and Caterpillar boots.

'What on earth are you doing here, Danny?'

'It's great to see you too!'

'Well?'

'I'm sorry Pete, I was with this guy earlier. He threw me out.'

'What do you mean, exactly?'

'It's a long story. Can I come in?'

Pete hesitated, wondering what he was going to do with the kid. The boy seemed a little crestfallen.

'I won't be any bother, Pete. I can phone for a taxi, if you could lend me the fare. Or I could just crash on the couch?'

Pete wasn't sure what to do. He knew Danny couldn't be at the cottage after midnight. He had to get rid of him somehow but equally he couldn't just leave him freezing on the doorstep. Pete beckoned him in. 'This isn't the best time, Danny.'

Danny looked at him sharply. 'Oh, have you got

someone here? Christ, I'm sorry. I should go.'

Pete saw in Danny's eyes the offer wasn't genuine. 'No Danny, it's fine. There's no one here. Come on in. But you can't stay long.'

Pete's mind was racing. If he called a taxi for the boy, it wouldn't get here in time. He wondered if he should just tell him the truth.

'Oh, you've dropped your drink,' Danny said, lifting the tumbler from the rug. 'Shall I fix you another one? I could do with one myself after what I've been through.'

Pete nodded, only half listening. Danny poured two whiskies, handed one to Pete and looked at him quizzically. 'What's wrong Pete? You look like you've seen a ghost.'

'Not exactly.'

'You look ever so pale.' Danny brushed his hand against Pete's cheek. Pete gently moved his hand away. Then Danny noticed the fetish-doll lying on the table. 'Hey, what's this ugly thing?' He picked it up.

'It's nothing. Put it down.'

'Where did you get it? It's weird, kind of cool in a way.' Danny gazed at it strangely.

The fetish was already casting its spell. Pete took it from him and laid it back down. 'I have to tell you something,' Pete said. 'And there's not much time.'

The kid was still staring at the doll.

'Danny!'

'What's the matter? What's going on with you?'

Pete glanced at the wall clock. 11.15pm. No, that couldn't be right. The clock must have stopped. 'What time is it?' he asked.

'Time?' Danny looked at the clock on the wall. 'Isn't it quarter past eleven?'

'No.'

Frantically, Pete patted his pockets for his phone then saw it on the sideboard next to the whisky. He tapped the screen. The display flashed. Half past midnight. The room was suddenly horribly, ferociously cold. He went to the window and looked out over the woods. Nothing was moving in the dark.

'Please Danny, you've got to get out of here. Your life depends on it.'

Danny tilted his head slightly as Pete turned to look at him. Pete couldn't understand why the dumb kid wouldn't listen.

'Trust me, Danny. You have to go right now!'

'But this is exactly where I'm supposed to be.' Danny picked up the liverish red doll again. 'I can't go now. I've come this far to find you. And you've been expecting me all night.'

'He had a mop of thick, black hair and
his beard framed a strong jaw.'

HAIRY TALE

Panelling painted a dark sludge green, a stag's head, a fox, a pike in a glass case, an etching of druids in a circle of standing stones: the Valdemar was eccentric in a particularly Victorian way, and the only inn for miles around. The fireplace in the corner crackled and spat. I warmed my hands while Trent ordered the drinks. So far our trip to the Lakes had been less than perfect. The tent was smaller than I'd expected. Trudging over rocky slopes was not really my thing. I longed for a hot bath and a comfortable bed. Trent came over, juggling wine and crisps. He looked disapproving.

'Everything all right?' I said.

'Not next to the fire. It's the middle of July.' He looked around, then nodded towards another table.

Now we were sitting next to the toilets. Trent ripped open the crisp packet, sat back and folded his arms. 'Still sulking, Sam?'

'I'm not sulking. I'm just not a fan of camping. And neither are you. Admit it.'

'I'm having a great time.'

'That's not what you said when it took so long to pitch the tent.'

Trent snorted and looked away.

I drank some more wine. 'Who's sulking now?' I said.

'I'm just tired of your constant whining, that's all.'

'Perhaps they've got a room here? Just for one night?'

'We're not staying in a hotel. We said we'd try camping and that's what we're doing.'

I saluted.

'You really are unbelievable,' he said. 'You have to find fault with everything.'

'Admit you were wrong. Just once. We shouldn't have come up here. Neither of us is enjoying it.'

'I'm not wrong and I am enjoying it. You're the problem, not me.'

'What's that supposed to mean?'

'I have to sort out the tent while you just bumble around and get in the way.'

'But you won't let me help you. And whenever I try, you tell me I'm doing it all wrong.'

For a time, neither of us spoke.

'At least we tried it, didn't we?' I said. 'We did a

camping holiday.'

'The first of many.'

I rolled my eyes.

'Right!' Trent stood up decisively. 'I'm fed up with this. We're going back to the tent.'

'I'm not going anywhere. I like it here.'

'Fine!' He snatched up his cagoule and marched out.

I looked around the room. There was a guy sitting by the fireplace now. He raised an eyebrow as our eyes met. He was cute in a rough and ready way. He had a mop of thick, black hair and his beard framed a strong jaw. He beckoned to me and I went over.

'You're welcome to join me. I saw you sitting here earlier.'

'That's very kind. Thank you.' I noticed the thick dark hairs on the back of his outstretched hand.

'Bill.'

'Sam.'

He gripped my hand firmly. 'Where did the other guy go?'

'Back to the camp site.'

'Had a falling out?'

'You could say that.'

Bill scooched forward and pointed at the open crisp packet.

'Help yourself,' I said.

He filled his mouth with crisps and munched. Then he grabbed his bottle of beer, tilted his head back and chugged it down. I watched his Adam's apple bob up and down. Dark hairs sprouted over the neck of his black muscle tee. He smacked the bottle down and leaned forward. 'So, what brings you to the Lakes?'

'Well, me and my friend -'

'Boyfriend?'

'Yes, me and my boyfriend, we felt like a change. We've never been camping before.'

'But it's not going so well?'

I leaned forward, mirroring Bill's pose. 'We both hate it. Only he won't admit it.'

Bill laughed. 'So, what are you going to do with the rest of your evening?'

'Stay here. Let him cool off, then go back.'

'I'm famished,' Bill said.

He'd wolfed down most of the crisps by now. He leaned back in his chair, clasped his hands behind his head and spread his legs. I fought the urge to look between them. And lost.

'You wanna get a bite?' His stare was penetrating.

'Sure.' My voice cracked as I answered him. I cleared my throat. 'That'd be great.'

'Burger?'

'Yeah, that'll be fine.'

'How do you like it?'

'Well done.'

'My treat.'

Bill wandered over to the crowded bar, commanding the barman's attention immediately.

'Burgers are on their way. How long have you and

your boyfriend been up here?'

'We came up a couple of days ago. We go back the day after tomorrow.'

'You're not a fan of the great outdoors then?'

I shook my head. 'How about you? Are you the outdoor type?'

'Yes. It's in my blood.'

'I'm a townie at heart, I'm afraid. I like a nice warm bed.'

'The earth is a nice warm bed.'

The server brought the burgers. Bill had his rare. We didn't speak much as we ate. Bill wiped his mouth and finished his beer. 'Delicious. Your boyfriend's missing out.'

'There's plenty of tinned food back at the camp.'

'You don't seem too concerned about him.'

'He can take care of himself.' It was getting dark outside. 'I suppose I'd better be making a move.'

Bill raised his eyebrows. 'Where are you camped?'

'About twenty minutes away. Just beyond Lake Buttermere.'

'I'm not far from there. I'll walk with you.'

The lights of the pub faded rapidly behind us. Trees bordered either side of the path and the moonlight glimmered on the lake beyond.

'These lonely trails give me the creeps,' I said.

'Why?'

'I dunno. I start to imagine vampires, werewolves, that sort of thing.'

'There is a legend of a werewolf in these parts.

The wolf man of the Lakes.'

'Really?'

'Yeah. There've been sightings of him over the years. Always when the moon's full.'

'Have you ever seen him?'

'I've heard about plenty of encounters. Last year a couple of hikers strayed from the path into the uplands. One guy was mauled to death, the other got away to tell the tale.'

'Isn't that the beginning of *American Werewolf in London*?'

Bill laughed. He took my hand in his. 'Don't know. I've never seen it.'

'It's getting dark pretty quickly.'

'Look at the moon,' he said. 'So beautiful.'

The moon was low in the sky between dark wisps of cloud. Its light cast skittering shadows around us. I shuddered. Bill squeezed my hand.

'Can you smell the scent of the trees?'

'Not really.'

'It's something you get used to the more time you spend in the woodlands.'

'You spend a lot of time here?'

'Sure.'

'You didn't tell me what you did?'

'Woodsman.'

'And you've never seen the famous werewolf?'

Bill didn't reply. Moving with powerful strides, he took us away from the path. We broke through the woodland into a sandy clearing on the edge of the lake.

Bill beamed playfully. 'Fancy a swim?'

I was in way over my head with this guy. 'Sure. Why not?'

Bill kicked off his boots and peeled off his shirt, revealing a toned and hairy torso. He pulled down his jeans. He wore no underwear. I gazed at him as he splashed into the water and swam towards the middle of the lake. By the time I had undressed, he was waving to me from the distance. The water was cold as I waded in. I hoped Bill couldn't see me shivering. I swam out to meet him. His wet hair was glossy and his dark eyes sparkled in the moonlight.

'Cold?'

'Yes.'

'Come here.' He kissed me, his hands gliding over my skin. He reached between my legs. I reciprocated. We twisted and curved in the water, peaking at the same moment. Bodies entwined, we drifted in the blackness for a while then swam back to shore. We lay on our backs on the sand, staring up at the moon.

'Still worried about werewolves?'

'No.'

'They say that bathing naked in the moonlight can turn you into one.'

'Then I guess I'm a werewolf now.'

'But there's one surefire method.'

'What's that?'

'A medieval priest, Gervase of Tilbury, wrote that

rolling naked in the sand under the full moon was the surest way. Wanna try it?'

I laughed.

Bill turned over and over, caking himself in sand. I copied him. Then he climbed on top of me, grabbing my hair in his fist. He pulled my head back and nuzzled my neck, taking in my scent. Then he licked and kissed it. I ran my hands over his back feeling the soft hairs brush against my fingertips. He spat on his fingers and made me wet and then he pushed inside me. He moved in steady rhythm until I felt the surging of his heat. We stayed locked together for a while then he got to his feet. I got up too. With his back to me, Bill began to urinate on the sand.

I smiled. 'The call of nature?'

He turned and sprayed warm glittering gold towards me, catching my legs. 'Just marking my territory.'

I looked at the surrounding woods. For the first time I smelled the sweet balsamic scent of the fir trees. The moonlight's reflection on the lake brought everything to life. Suddenly Bill was at my shoulder.

'We'd better go. Your boyfriend will wonder where you are.'

I nodded. I didn't want to go. I wanted to forget about Trent and stay here forever. I wanted to swim in the lake, make love in the sand and run naked through the trees. Most of all I wanted Bill. We dressed and walked in silence along the trail. Tree cover blackened the path but Bill guided us. When we came to a fork in the road, he pointed to the higher ground.

'I'm up there.'

'Then this is where we part company. Will I see you again?'

'Maybe.'

'Well, at least I didn't meet any werewolves.'

Bill gave me a mischievous look, a final kiss, and he was gone.

'Discover the date
of your own death.'

EXPIRY DATE

APRIL 23RD

5.16pm

A skull and crossbones, weeping blood theatrically, flickered in the middle of the screen. The caption flashed: 'Discover the date of your own death.' Carl's finger hovered over the mouse pad.

'Go on,' Danny squeezed his arm. 'Do it.'

'You do it.'

'Not me - you know I'm superstitious.'

'It's just a load of bunkum, Dan. *Expirydate.com.* Even the name's a joke. And what does it say here?'

Carl clicked the *about* icon and columns of text appeared in a flowery font.

'This website is encoded with incantations from the Rite of Marchosias, one of Hell's most powerful invocations. The site's founder, Donald J. Parker, made a pact with the demon Marchosias to bring this website to the world. Do you dare to enter?'

Carl snorted, 'What a load of crap.'

'So go on, big guy. Click enter.'

'There's no way some kooky website can really predict the day you're going to die.'

'Then there's nothing to worry about. Go on.'

Danny leaned into Carl, the scent of his skin like warm honeycomb, his hand over Carl's hand, guiding his fingers. Carl felt himself stirring. The next page appeared.

'There!' Danny's cornflower blue eyes were puckish. 'You're in.'

He gently punched Carl's shoulder and leaned back in his chair, watching him. Danny's abs were outlined in his satiny white tee. Carl dragged his gaze back to the computer screen.

'All right,' he said. 'Here goes nothing.'

'Do you enter of your own free will?' Danny asked.

Carl thought it an odd question.

'Indeed I do.' He put on his best ghostly voice.

He read the instructions: 'Enter full name, date of birth, ethnicity, height, weight, eye colour and mother's maiden name.'

His fingers worked the keyboard in rapid clicks.

'Interesting how it doesn't want to know anything about my actual health, like whether I'm a smoker, or how much alcohol I drink,' Carl said. 'Nothing of any real use in predicting someone's longevity.'

'Maybe there are other ways of determining a person's fate,' Danny suggested.

'Yeah right, like the star you were born under, I suppose?'

'Why not?'

'Oh come on Danny. None of that has any basis in science and neither does this dumb website.'

Carl didn't know why he felt uneasy as he moved the cursor to the final icon: *Your expiry date*.

'Ready?' Danny grinned.

Carl clicked the mouse pad. And stared at the screen incredulously.

'What the hell?' he said.

The date of his death was given as 23rd of April - today's date - ten years in the future. Carl entered his details again. The same date flashed up again.

'How on earth can it say that?' He heard his voice rising. He was only thirty-five and he planned on living way beyond his forties.

'Hey, it's not my fault,' Danny said.

Carl closed the web page and glared at the empty screen.

'Stupid bloody website.'

*

79

12.01am

Danny Alexander was the last person Carl expected to hear from. Why was he texting after all these years, and on this of all days? Carl opened the message.

Know what day it is? Dx

Yes, I do. Sooo gr8 to hear from u. How r u? Cx

R u scared? Dx

If I'm honest, just a little. Crazy isn't it? Where r u? Want 2 meet up? Cxx

I'll c u soon. Dxx

OK when? Cxxx

Danny didn't reply.

07.01am

Carl had decided to stay awake for the full twenty-four hours. He didn't want to die in his sleep. He sat up all night watching TV and drinking coffee. Now, he was cleaning out the percolator and listening to the news on the radio. He noticed a wasp crawling across the outside of the window and banged hard on the glass to frighten it away.

08.13am

He took a shower, feet spread squarely on the cubicle floor. He towelled himself and made sure his feet were bone dry before stepping out onto the bathroom tiles. He got dressed and stretched out on the bed, wondering how he was going to get through an entire day just doing nothing. He went downstairs gingerly, made tea and toast, and surfed some satellite channels.

10.37am

He must have dozed off. His arm trailed on the floor and his body lay awkwardly on the sofa. His back ached, so did his bladder. He went upstairs to pee, holding onto the banister carefully as he made his way up and down. He decided it might be better to pee in a bucket just for today. There was one in the garden shed and on his way to fetch it, he kept his eyes on the ground, watching for uneven or loose paving stones.

1.12pm

Lunchtime. He had to escape from the living room - he couldn't sit through another episode of *Midsomer Murders*. So far so good - no life-threatening injuries. He checked the fridge and decided it was better to steer clear of leftovers like salmon or chicken. And better to avoid using sharp knives too. He opened a fresh loaf of sliced bread, using a butter knife to spread a thick layer of peanut butter and raspberry jam.

He reach for a mug. It fell onto the counter, rolled off the side and, before he could catch it, smashed on the floor. Cursing himself, he fetched the dustpan and brush and carefully swept up the broken pieces. Then he vacuumed the floor. He rolled the hoover

over and over the spot to make sure nothing sharp was left. He checked there were no cuts on his hands and washed them thoroughly.

3.47pm

A knock at the door. Carl had made sure no deliveries were coming today. He turned the sound down on the TV and sat rigid on the sofa. The knock came again. He felt a tightness in his throat. Please go away. Now there was someone standing at the window looking in: his elderly next door neighbour, Mibsy.

'Oh you are in. Oh thank goodness!' Her voice was muffled through the glass. Carl walked over.

'What's the matter, Mibsy? Is everything all right?'

'It's Furby, he's got himself into the most awful mess.'

'Oh?'

'He's up on the garage roof, dear. Might I trouble you to come and get him down?'

Dread scuttered through Carl's body.

'Okay. I'll be right out.'

He grabbed his grippiest trainers and opened the door.

'Oh, I'm so grateful,' Mibsy said. 'I honestly have no idea how he got up there. He didn't come in this afternoon, you see. Hadn't touched his Whiskas.'

'His whiskers?'

'His lunch. His bowl was full, and his saucer of milk too, and no sign of him.'

She led Carl round to her garage where a dumpy grey tomcat was perched nervously at the apex of the tiled roof.

'Come on Furby,' Carl said, stretching out his arms and wiggling his fingers in encouragement.

'Oh, he won't jump, dear. You'll have to go up and get him. There's a small ladder in the garage.'

Carl brushed the cobwebs off the ladder and carried it outside. He climbed carefully up to roof level and reached out for the cat. The cat backed away.

'You'll have to get right up onto the roof and grab him,' Mibsy said. 'Show him who's boss.'

Carl gripped the vertex of the roof and pulled himself up. Then he flattened himself against the sloping tiles, heels wedged into the guttering for support. Furby retreated further. Carl slid cautiously along the roof, reaching up as the cat attempted to scurry past him. Carl grabbed it, scooping it off the roof and in towards his shoulder. The cat clung on, digging in its claws. Carl backed slowly towards the ladder, easing himself outwards, bottom first, one foot on the top rung, then the other, and climbed down. His heart was thumping in his chest as he handed the cat back to Mibsy.

'Oh, thank you. Thank you so much,' she said.

'No problem.' Carl's voice came out a little strangled, his throat was dry.

'Would you like to come in for a cuppa?'

'That's very nice of you, Mibsy, but I'd better get

back.' Carl put the ladder away and hurried home, closing and double locking the door behind him. Head in hands, he slid down the wall to the floor. Why was he letting this superstitious nonsense get to him? He wanted a drink then decided it was better to keep a clear head, at least until midnight. Then he could drink as much as he liked.

6.43pm

The living room was chilly. Carl put down his magazine. He checked the log basket by the stove. It was empty. He found his torch and went out to the garden. He bundled up enough logs to get through the evening and took them back inside, dropping them into the basket. He put a fire lighter and some kindling inside the stove, placed a couple of logs on top, and struck a match. The fire lighter blazed into life and Carl shut the hatch, twisting open the vent.

8.31pm

Carl's dinner was easy and risk-free, a simple risotto ready meal which he heated in the microwave. He scooped the piping-hot mixture onto his plate and settled down to a documentary about the history of the jumbo jet. There were less than four hours of the day left and he was feeling more relaxed. He decided to have a glass of wine after all. Then he had another. Changing channels, he found an old Dracula film, and an exquisite drowsiness began to enfold him.

Carl sat up. Dracula had given way to a programme about Winchester Cathedral. The logs had burnt out but the room was still warm. He checked the time: 11.52. Eight minutes until the 24th. And safety. All that apprehension had been for nothing. How could he have taken that website seriously for even a minute? He felt a complete wuss. He decided to text Danny, tell him he'd made it through the day, maybe suggest going for a drink. As he scrolled through his messages, he caught sight of something dark as it rose up out of the log basket. He dropped his phone as the queen wasp flew towards him, buzzing angrily. He swiped at it with a magazine and its buzz got louder and higher. Then it dived suddenly and stung him on the neck. He swiped at it again and this time he hit it into the wall. It fell onto the floor and he stamped on it, squashing it, once and for all, into the floorboard.

Now he felt the tightening in his chest. His fingers found the swelling on his neck around the sting. His throat felt thick and it hurt when he swallowed. He realised he was having to fight for breath. His vision blurred and his heart began to flutter like a bird. He fell forwards onto the floor and his fingers closed around his phone. He tried to enter the pass code and call 999, but his hand was numb. His body began to shudder uncontrollably and then, abruptly, his heart stopped.

It was 11.59. And he had wanted to stay alive.

The young man stood at the window and looked down at Carl's dead body. Danny hadn't aged a day in the decade that had passed. A saurian smile played gently across his lips, then, hands in pockets, he turned and walked slowly away.

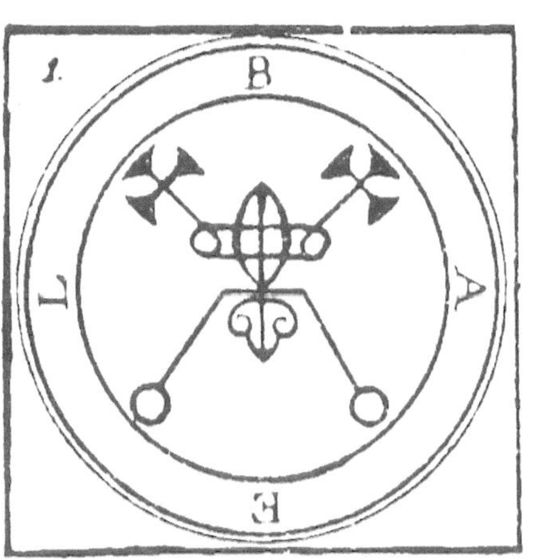
1.
B
A
E
L

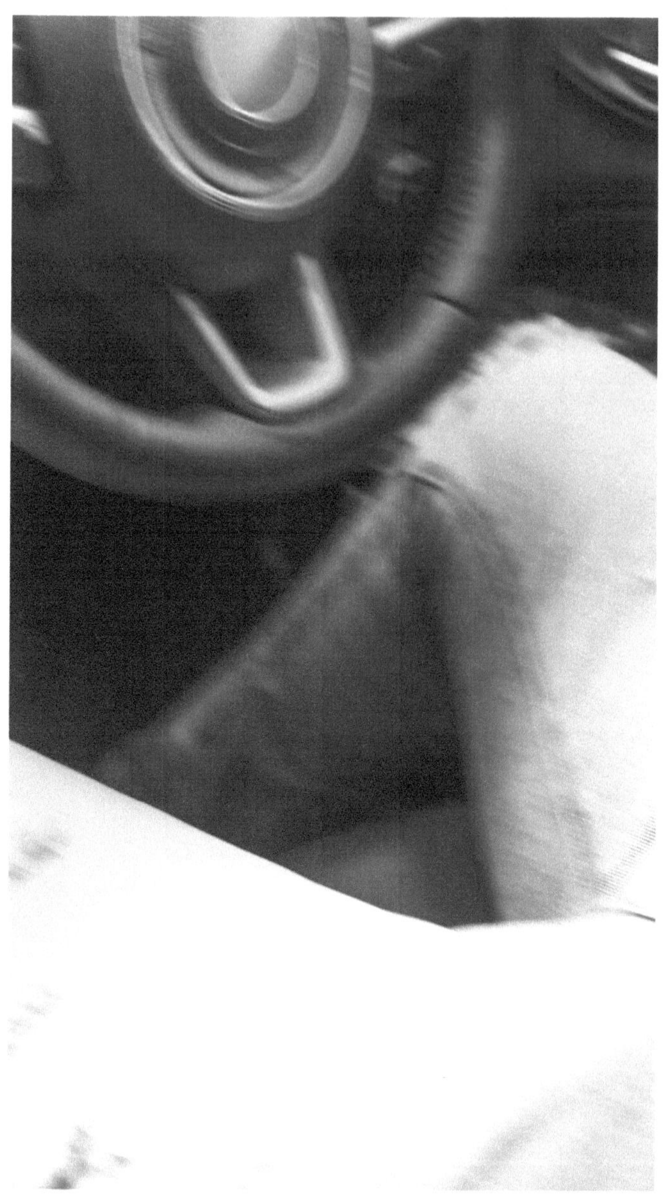

'Ben began to relax as he contemplated the
empty country lane winding ahead of them.'

RUN!

'Please, don't do this,' Aaron sobbed.

His elder brother, Isaac, was holding him in a half-nelson. Pain seared across the back of his head and he thought his arm was going to break.

Father Tully advanced, pressing his crucifix against Aaron's head. The priest's voice was thick with religious feeling as he spoke the incantation: *Omnipotens Domine, Verborum Dei Patris, Christe Jesu, Deus et Dominus universae creaturae…*

He turned to Isaac with a simple instruction. 'Now.'

Isaac forced Aaron into the brimming bathtub. Aaron's father forced his head under the surface. The freezing water stung Aaron's eyes, filled his nostrils, poured down the back of his throat. He struggled but his father's grip held him under.

Then he was hauled up, coughing and choking. Isaac pulled him up so roughly it sent shooting pain along the length of his spine.

'Begone Satan!' the priest denounced. '*Ecce crucem Domini, fugite partes adversae. Vicit leo de tribu Juda, radix David.* Force the Devil out, almighty Lord.'

Aaron was thrust under again. The water seemed to slow time. He felt almost peaceful, separated briefly from the madness of the world above. He was hauled up again, and plunged back into the water.

…Audi ergo, et time, satana, inimice fidei, hostis generis humani, mortis adductor, vitae raptor…

Aaron felt his lungs were going to explode.

…justitae declinator, malorum radix, fomes vitorum, seductor hominum, proditor gentium…

Fear rose up sharply from his gut, tore through him. If only Ben were here. He needed Ben.

*

Ben watched the three men from the darkness of the hallway. It had been easy enough to get into the house through a downstairs window. Now Father Tully was leading a prayer session, reading from the Gospel of St. Matthew. Isaac and Aaron's father knelt in front of the priest, hands clasped in supplication to a higher power.

Everyone knew the Taylors were a fanatically religious family. Aaron's mother had died a year before during one of Isaac's psychotic meltdowns.

Her husband had been left to raise his sons the only way he knew how, with the Bible and the strap.

Mr Taylor had taken Aaron out of the sixth form because he suspected he was getting too close to one of the other boys. He had beaten him in an attempt to get at the truth, hired a tutor from their church, confiscated the boy's phone, and now monitored his emails. He had pleaded with Father Tully to steer his son away from the 'path of damnation'.

Ben joined Aaron's Bible class just so they could see each other. Aaron would complain of feeling ill and Ben would take him outside for air. They'd kiss and talk of running away. When Isaac was released from the psychiatric hospital, Ben was concerned things would get bad for Aaron. He had been right. Tonight, he would take Aaron away for good.

*

Aaron had been left bound and unconscious on the bathroom floor. His blond hair was sodden and lay in pale streaks across his face. His white tee shirt and jeans were soaked with water. There were cuts and bruises on his hands and feet. Ben untied him and touched his face to wake him.

'Ben… you're here.'

'Yes, darling. I'm taking you away tonight. Somewhere where they can't hurt you.'

Ben pressed his lips against Aaron's forehead,

91

holding him close for a few moments before they made their way silently downstairs. The prayer session was in full swing. Mr Taylor's keys were on the kitchen table. Aaron showed him which one opened the back door. Ben twisted the key in the lock.

'Take your dirty paws off my son, you black bastard!' Mr Taylor was standing behind them, fists clenched, eyes wild, like an animal. Father Tully came in behind him, Bible in hand, glowering at Ben.

'So, you're the one who has led this innocent child along the path of evil. You must answer to your Lord and master, boy.'

Aaron's father advanced towards his son and Ben blocked his path.

'Let us go, Mr. Taylor. You can't stop us.'

'Yes I can.'

The huge man lunged at Ben, grabbing him by the throat and slamming him against the wall. He tightened his fingers around Ben's throat. Ben kicked out at him but couldn't break free. He thought he was going to pass out. The next thing he knew there was a loud thud and Aaron's father was slumped on top of him, crushing him against the wall. Ben felt himself being dragged from underneath, then Aaron was leaning over him: 'You all right?'

'Yeah, I guess.'

The room began to swim back into focus. Aaron's

father was moaning and clutching the back of his head. Father Tully was intoning: 'And the Devil who had deceived them was thrown into the lake of fire and sulphur where the beast and the false prophet were, and they will be tormented day and night forever and ever.'

'We're taking your dad's car!' Ben told Aaron.

They tore along the driveway, the sound of yelling behind them. Aaron jumped into the passenger seat. Ben fired up the engine and threw the gears into reverse. Aaron's father was running at them. The car hurtled back along the driveway as the bear-like man leaped onto the bonnet, frantic with rage. The car spun out onto the main road and Aaron's father was thrown sideways, his body smacking onto the tarmac.

'Devil!' Father Tully screamed as the car raced away down the empty lane.

*

Aaron put his hand on Ben's thigh. 'Ease down a bit.'

Ben took his foot off the accelerator and looked at Aaron. How beautiful he was. 'We're gonna be okay. They can't hurt you anymore.'

'I know.'

'It's only about twenty minutes to Taunton. We can stay with my sister for a couple of days till we figure things out.'

'We have kind of stolen my dad's car though, Ben.

What are we going to do?'

'We'll think of something. You look shattered. Try to get some sleep. I'll wake you up when we…'

Isaac launched himself at Aaron from the back seat of the car. His face livid and manic. Ben slammed on the brakes. The car juddered violently and skidded to an abrupt halt. Ben and Aaron scrambled out. They stood looking at each other, not knowing what to do next.

From the car: no movement, no sound.

Ben walked back cautiously and looked in the window. Isaac was curled awkwardly against the front seat. Ben eased the door open slowly. 'Hey.'

Ben threw a doubtful look at Aaron. Aaron bent over the car.

'Isaac?'

His brother sprang suddenly like a rabid cat and Aaron staggered back. He spat and clawed at Ben, jabbed a fist into Ben's face and Ben's nose started to bleed.

'Aaron, get in the car!'

Ben raised his hands to protect himself as Isaac hissed and punched. He managed to get hold of Isaac's elbows and push him forcefully to the ground. He ran to the car and floored the accelerator. 'Aaron, are you all right. Did he hurt you?'

'I'm fine.'

'Thank God.'

'No need to thank him.'

Not a soul for miles around. Ben began to relax as he contemplated the empty country road winding ahead of them. He'd done it. He'd got Aaron out of there. They were safe. The car's headlights picked up the spiny outlines of bare trees in the darkness. A road sign loomed up out of the shadows. Eighteen miles to Taunton. Ben looked over at Aaron. He was staring straight ahead. 'Aaron, you okay?'

Aaron started to chuckle.

'What's so funny?'

Aaron didn't answer. His chuckling turned ugly. Ben had never heard him laugh that way before.

'Why are you laughing like that?'

Aaron eased his hand between Ben's legs.

'What if it were true? What if they were right all along? What if I really am the Devil?'

'Mayday. Mayday. This is the
two-man trawler Jilly Jones.'

BENEATH THE SURFACE

'Mayday. Mayday. This is the two-man trawler Jilly Jones, five miles out from Cromer. Our engines are dead. We are adrift. Request assistance. Over.'

'Anything?'

'No. Nothing.'

'This isn't looking good, Joe.'

'Nonsense, lad. We haven't been out here that long.'

'It feels like hours. What if we end up drifting out towards the wind farm? We'll be smashed to pieces.'

'Come on now, Billy. You know Old Silas will realise something's up when we don't get back. He'll raise the alarm and the coast guard will be out in no time.'

'I guess you're right.'

'I am.'

'It's eerie without the engine, drifting in the dark.'

'At least the sea's calm tonight.'

'But it's so dark.'

'No moon.'

'Joe, what if no one comes?'

'They will come.'

'But you can't even raise anyone on the radio.'

'They will come. Try not to fret so.'

'I'm glad it's you I'm with, Joe.'

'Why's that, then?'

'I reckon if things start to get bad, you'll get us out of it.'

'I couldn't save Freddy.'

'No, but you wouldn't let that happen to me.'

'Things won't get bad, Billy. We'll be fine.'

'What if we're not? You didn't expect the Kingfisher to go down.'

'No… No, I didn't. But no use dredging up bad memories. This is nothing like that night.'

'Was Freddy the same age as me?'

'Give or take.'

'It's terrible. He was so young.'

'Stop thinking about it.'

'Sorry, Joe… I just… I can't help wondering what he'd be doing now.'

'Me too.'

'He didn't get much of a go at life.'

'Sometimes shit just happens, Billy. There's no reasoning why.'

'I'd hate to die without saying some of the things I need to say to people.'

'You're not going to die. You're just a kid. You haven't lived, haven't seen anything of life. What things have you got to say, Billy?'

'There are things. Things I need to be honest about. Just things I need to say, that's all.'

'I'm sure the people close to you know you love them. They don't need telling.'

'It's not that. It's about me. Lies about me.'

'Who's been telling lies about you?'

'It's me. I've been telling lies about myself, hiding who I really am.'

'Who are you then? Davey Jones come to drag me down to the bottom of the sea?'

'You're making fun of me.'

'I'm sorry, Bill. Go on. What is it you want to say?'

'If we make it back, there are things people don't know about me.'

'Something's been eating away at you for months, I know that much. Sometimes it seems you're a million miles away, not here with the rest of us.'

'It's difficult to get the words out. I've never told anybody before.'

'Just say it. I won't throw you overboard.'

'I don't like girls, Joe. I like boys.'

'Oh.'

'Yes, oh.'

'Well, that's your business, nobody else's.'

'But I want it to be other people's business. I don't

want to hide away. I don't want to pretend I'm someone that I'm not.'

'That may not be so easy. Folk can be unkind.'

'I can't go on lying. Nobody wants to live and die with some great big secret, do they?'

'I'm going try the radio again. Mayday. Mayday. This is the trawler Jilly Jones, five miles out from Cromer. Our engines are dead. We are adrift. Request assistance. Over.'

'Still nothing?'

'No.'

'Joe, what is it? Are you disgusted by me?'

'No, don't be daft. It's not that.'

'Something's wrong.'

'I'm okay.'

'No you're not. I'm sorry. I shouldn't have said anything. I've made things awkward.'

'No, Billy. It's not that, honest. It's good to get things off your chest. God knows, we've each of us got some secret or other. There's something I've never told anyone about the night Freddy drowned. The sinking didn't happen the way folk think.'

'What happened really?'

'We should never have gone out that night, Billy. I thought we'd get back before the storm hit but we left it too late. Then, when the storm came, the waves were so high. Fifteen feet or more. They kept on coming. We were tossed about like a cork. I kept hoping, praying we would make it. Then the boat smashed apart. It all happened so fast. Suddenly I was clinging to a piece of hull, barely able to keep my head above water, calling Freddy's name in the dark. Next thing I knew, he was there beside me, grabbing at me, terrified. He was in a blind panic, struggling like an animal. He was dragging us both under. I was gulping down water. I couldn't breathe, couldn't get any air. I kept pleading with him to calm down. He just kept on thrashing around, pulling me under...'

'Go on.'

'I knew he was going to drown us both... I had no choice.... I managed to get him off me... And the sea took him.'

'Oh God, Joe.'

'I killed him, Billy.'

'No. No, you didn't. It's like you said. He was panicking so much there was nothing you could do. You would've both died.'

'It would've been better.'

'You can't blame yourself. Nobody knows what they'd do in a situation like that.'

'Maybe, but I can't - '

'Joe, what was that?'

'I didn't hear anything.'

'Listen!'

'It sounds like church bells.'

'God, Joe! It's the bells of Shipden.'

'Come off it, Billy. I don't believe in that nonsense and neither should you.'

'Plenty say it's true.'

'Then plenty are fools. Shipden is just a myth.'

'The sound of a sunken bell is a warning that someone's going to die.'

'Where did you hear that rubbish? There aren't any bloody bells. Stop talking about it Billy. You're scaring yourself.'

'Christ, Joe! What was that?!'

'Sounded like something banging against the hull.'

'There it is again.'

'A piece of drift wood, maybe.'

'There's something else. It sounds like something's climbing onto the bow.'

'Don't be daft!'

'Something's trying to get onto the boat!'

'Get a hold of yourself, boy! Wait here...'

'... Joe? Is there anything there?'

'It's pretty dark. Difficult to make out much.'

'What can you see?'

'No. It can't be.'

'Joe? What is it?'

'This can't be real'

'Joe, what's going on?'

'Stay back there Billy, don't look.'

'What d'you mean? I'm coming up to see.'

'No, Billy. Don't.'

'... Oh God, what is that?'

'It's him.'

'Him?'

'It's Freddy. Or what's left of him.'

'Joe, what are you doing? Stay away from it!'

'It's me you want, isn't it Freddy? Leave the boy. Take me, not him.'

'Joe, don't go near it!"

'I'm sorry, Billy. I have to.'

'Don't leave me, Joe. Please, don't leave me here in the dark.'

*'This guy of yours must be
some kind of psycho.'*

MY FUNNY VALENTINE

The card was lying on the mat when Ishani came downstairs. On the front was a wide-eyed black cat with its hair standing on end. Inside it said: 'Don't be a scaredy cat, just be my Valentine.' Then, handwritten: 'Meet me in the graveyard at midnight.' She made herself a coffee, showered and dressed.

By the time she got to the shoot, the photographer was already set up. She had worked with him several times before. And every time, he came on to her. He was much older than most of the photographers she worked with. He came from an era of bottom pinching and Page Three stunners. Unfortunately, today, she was modelling lingerie.

'You're looking delightful as ever, Ishani.'

'Thank you.'

'Lay out on the bed for me, darling. That's right. Turn your head to the left slightly. Perfect.' The shutter produced a rapid succession of clicks. 'Lean forward, show me some booty. Absolutely mint, my love.'

After a couple of hours they took a break.

'So, what's a hot babe like you doing on Valentine's Day?'

'Nothing special.'

'Come on, you must have dozens of blokes lining up to take you out.'

'Not really. I'm having a quiet night in with an old movie.'

'Not even a box of chocolates?'

'Only if I buy it myself.'

After the break, he was all over her. Fingers tugging at her bra, hitching up her briefs, trailing unnecessarily over her thighs. 'Just need to be a little more revealing there, darling. A bit more eastern promise. That's lovely.'

'I can adjust these things myself, Rob.'

'Of course. Sorry, sweetheart. Force of habit. Guess I just can't keep my hands off you.'

By the time the session was over, Ishani had had enough. As soon as she got home she took a long hot shower. She wanted to wash everywhere Rob had touched. For the rest of the afternoon she made herself busy hoovering, paying some bills online, packing for a shoot in Bali the following week.

After dinner, she picked out her favourite evening

dress, styled and lacquered her hair and did her makeup. The doorbell rang. It was half past nine. She found Rob standing on the doorstep, a Paul A. Young selection in one hand, a bottle of Cristal in the other.

'I just couldn't let you be on your own on Valentine's.' He thrust his gifts into Ishani's hands and pushed past her. He reeked of beer. 'Hello, hello. What's this?' He picked up the Valentine's card. 'So you do have a date tonight, you naughty girl.' He opened it up. 'Oh, I see.'

'What do you see, Rob?'

'Well, it's obvious. Meet you in the graveyard? This guy of yours must be some kind of psycho. You need me to look after you, darling.'

'I don't need anyone to look after me.'

'He obviously knows where you live. I'll stay here tonight. Make sure you're okay.' He grabbed the Cristal. 'Be an angel and get us some glasses?'

'Rob, I really think you should go.'

'Oh come on, gorgeous. Relax and have a nice glass of champers with old Robbie.'

'I didn't ask you to come over.'

'I know, but I'm here now. Come on, love. Just one little drink, what's the harm?'

'Then you'll go?'

'Scouts honour.'

Rob gave a Fred Scuttle salute. 'You know I've never really understood you, Ishani.'

'Why's that?'

'You are one of the top models in the country, if not the world, and you don't seem to have a love life. Or at least you say you don't.'

'I've decided to concentrate on my career for now.'

Rob poured the drinks then slid his arms around Ishani's waist. 'I bet I could change your mind.'

She twisted away from him. He followed her into the next room. 'You and me, babe. We could be so good together.'

'Look Rob, you need to take it down a notch.'

'Come on, darling. You know you can't resist the old Robster.' He grabbed her and tried to kiss her. She thrust her hand between his mouth and hers.

'Just get off me, will you?'

'God, you're a cold bitch.'

'I'm not interested in you, Rob.'

He seized her shoulders and pushed her up against the wall. He groped her breasts as she squirmed in his grip. 'A bit of Robbie loving will warm you up.'

He stuck his tongue in her ear and she kneed him in the groin. 'What the fuck's wrong with you?'

Ishani marched to the front door and swung it open. 'Get out, Rob. Now.'

'My pleasure. You don't know what you're missing.'

'Oh, I think I do.'

'Frigid fucking lesbo. I'll leave you to your box set of *The L Word*!'

She kicked the door shut behind him. He had ripped her dress so she went upstairs and changed. Then she drank some of the Cristal. No reason to let good champagne go to waste. She browsed through a few TV channels and found a Joan Crawford and Cliff Robertson film about a woman who falls for a younger man. The film focused on the age barrier between them, and the young man's psychosis. She left the house half an hour before midnight, planning to take a slow walk to the cemetery.

The street lamps cast amber pools on the shiny pavements. The air carried a mild chill as she made her way past rows of dark houses. Along the high street, restaurants were crammed with doting couples at candlelit tables. The whole world seemed to be celebrating. Ishani turned onto the lonely lane that led to the cemetery beyond the cricket club. Overgrown gravestones sat among tall grasses that whispered in the wind. The funerary statues were like grey corpses wrapped in blankets of shadow. At the far end, a single wooden bench overlooked the graveyard. Ishani sat down. It was almost midnight. She breathed in the cool night air. A barn owl swooped in a flash of white before gliding up towards the treetops. She felt an icy breeze on the back of her neck then a cold hand on her shoulder. Christa was standing over her. She lifted Ishani and kissed her on the lips. Her long blonde hair was soft against Ishani's cheek as she caressed the back of her neck. 'It's been a long time,' Christa said.

'Too long. I've missed you.'

'This is how it has to be. Did you like the card?'

'Very funny.'

'What have you been doing with your life?'

'The usual. Photo shoots, interviews, drinking bottled water and eating lettuce. You know the sort of thing. How about you?'

Christa kissed Ishani's cheek. 'It's better if you don't know.'

'I wish we could meet more often.'

'We discussed this before.'

'I know, things are complicated. Things are always complicated!'

'I have to be very careful. That will never change. But we didn't come here to talk.' Christa wrapped her arms tight around Ishani. She kissed her throat and breasts as she held her. Suddenly there was a blinding light. And another. And another. Rob shot a whole roll of film on motor wind. Ishani shielded her face with her hands against the flash.

'Gotcha!' he sneered jubilantly.

'For God's sake, Rob. What the hell are you doing here?' Ishani said.

'I was just a little curious. Wanted to see if you were really meeting some guy at the graveyard. And look what I found, you and your lady love.'

Christa spoke to Ishani, ignoring Rob. 'Who is this man?'

'The photographer I was working with today.'

'He is a fool.'

'Hey! I'm standing right here, you know. Maybe you should think twice about calling me names, darling. I could easily end your girlfriend's career.'

Christa moved towards him. He took a step back.

'How would you do that?'

'If the press find out the lovely Ishani Kapoor likes girls, it'll finish her. I could make sure your little romance gets splashed all over the tabloids.'

'The world may be more enlightened than you think,' Christa said.

'Maybe, maybe not. Would you like to put it to the test?' He directed this question at Ishani. She went to Christa's side and took her hand.

'What exactly do you want, Rob? You're after more than a scoop for the *Daily Mail.*'

He scratched his nose. 'You're very astute, my love.'

'Well?'

'I want thirty grand in cash and you to make me your photographer of choice.'

'How do I do that? I don't book the sessions.'

'A top model can get anything she wants.'

'I want the negatives.'

'No can do, gorgeous. They're my insurance policy.'

Christa put her arm around Ishani's shoulders. 'Perhaps we should give him what he wants,' she said.

'What?!'

'As he says, it could be disastrous for you if those

pictures got out.'

Ishani couldn't believe what she was hearing. 'Maybe if I just came out publicly, it might make me more famous, more successful,' she said.

'Or it could destroy you. We can't take that risk.'

'You should listen to your girlfriend,' Rob told her, stroking his camera.

Christa softened her tone. 'Surely there is one other thing you want, Mr…?'

'Jones, Rob Jones.'

'Mr Jones. How about a little threesome, tonight? I mean, two women, and you, in a graveyard. It could be quite a thrill. Don't you think?'

'Oh come on, Christa,' Ishani said.

'It'll be all right, darling. We could look at it as a way of beginning our relationship with Mr. Jones.'

Rob began to unbutton his shirt. Christa fondled the front of his trousers. She guided Ishani's hand to his chest. Reluctantly Ishani began to caress him. He pushed both women down onto the grass. Christa slid from under him so he was on top of Ishani. Ishani could feel him hard against her. She turned her head away and screwed her eyes shut as he moved his hands over her breasts and licked her neck. He grabbed her chin and turned her back to face him, forcing his tongue into her mouth. She opened her eyes to see Christa grab Rob's hair and pull his head backwards. She snarled and buried her teeth in his neck, putting her hand over his mouth to silence his scream. He trembled and spasmed as she drank.

She pushed his lifeless body aside. Then she was on top of Ishani, kissing her. Ishani could taste the blood in Christa's mouth. They tumbled as Christa pulled her closer. They undressed and explored each other's nakedness, fingers and tongues finding soft hidden places. They moved together, blending into each other, cresting as one. Afterwards they lay in silence and listened to the chattering of foxes. Christa got up first. 'Time for me to leave.'

'So soon?'

'I have a long way to go and I have to be back before sunrise.'

Ishani nodded at Rob's corpse. 'What about him?'

'I'll take care of him.'

Christa picked him up as if he weighed nothing and carried him into the trees. When she came back Ishani was dressed and waiting for her. Christa handed her Rob's camera.

'You know every year I'll get a little older,' Ishani said.

'I'll still love you.'

'But one day I'll be seventy. And you won't have aged at all.'

Christa pressed a finger against Ishani's lips. 'Don't think about that now. Go and get your beauty sleep.'

Christa went with her as far as the road then dissolved into the night.

In the high street, Ishani watched a young couple

laughing, arm in arm, as she made her way
back home.

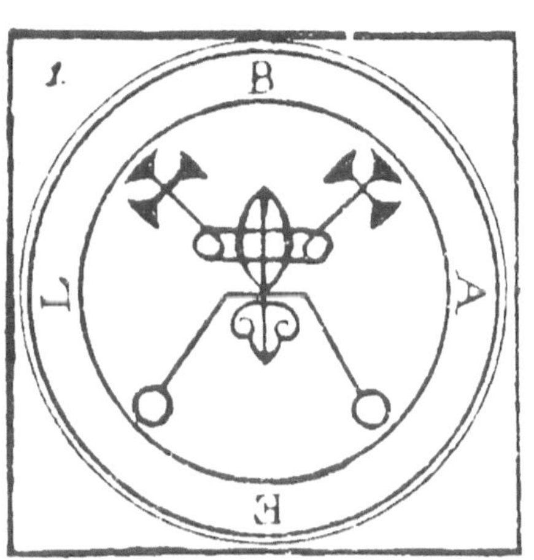
1.
B
A
L
E

*'They were pulling on the cable of my phone
charger wound tight around my throat.'*

THE MUDDLERS

Ever wondered why you're always left with one odd sock from the wash? Or why your headphone leads get so impossibly tangled? Or why your keys end up in the oddest places? These things are the work of the muddlers. They mess stuff up to irritate us, then feast on our frustration. They're always watching, always waiting. 'How do I know this?' you ask. Because I've seen them.

I've always been a meditation nut. I attended classes twice a week at the London Buddhist centre. I had the Headspace app and I'd read everyone on the subject from Jon Kabat-Zinn to Eckhart Tolle. Every evening I did breathing and relaxation exercises. Over time I began to break into new levels of consciousness. I found myself gazing down at my physical body from above. And that's when I first saw a muddler. He was about eight inches tall, plump, hairless and luminous blue. He was stuffing my door keys between the seat cushion and the side of my chair. Suddenly I was back in my body again and I couldn't see him anywhere. When I went back to my meditation he was gone.

As my practice developed, I experimented moving my disembodied awareness around my flat. That's when I spotted the muddler again. This time he had brought a friend. They were in the bedroom, twisting and knotting up the cord on my hairdryer. Their fingers were short blue spikes and they moved like lightning. Whenever I entered this heightened meditative state, I caught them red-handed. I watched them drop my wallet behind the sofa, crease up sheets on the airer, hide my reading glasses. Whenever I couldn't find the cap for my toothpaste or I misplaced my signet ring, I reckoned the muddlers were up to their mischief again. Soon, if I simply relaxed my breathing and softened my gaze, I was able see them.

At my local cafe, I tried my breathing trick and there they were - more muddlers. I watched as they mixed up the waitress's till receipts. At first she was confused, and then she had an almighty row with a customer. As the argument heated up, the muddlers absorbed the energy of the conflict through their outstretched spike-fingers. Their bodies glowed and puffed up. Next they slid a young woman's shopping bag out of sight so she left without it. Five minutes later, she came running back and they absorbed her nervous energy. I watched two muddlers on the Underground swing on a woman's shoulder bag as she dropped her oyster card into it. The card missed the bag and fell on the ground as she dashed for the escalator. In a packed carriage, a muddler leaned over a teenage couple as they kissed. He weaved strands of the girl's hair into the zip of her boyfriend's jacket. As she pulled away, her hair was ripped out at the roots. As the weeks passed, I observed more and more muddler mischief. They blocked up toilets, pulled money out of trouser pockets, unplugged phone chargers and pushed the shut down button on computers. Every time there was anger, conflict or frustration, they fed on it like ravenous piglets at a sow's teat.

*

I had not seen my muddlers for a while and I was beginning to think they'd moved on to pastures new. Then, as my awareness was floating above my living room, I saw them pushing a bottle of vodka towards the edge of the kitchen counter. I swooped back into my body, jumped up and put the bottle away. When I resumed my meditation - softening my gaze - my muddlers were staring at me with hands on hips and contemptuous expressions. Now they knew I could see them. They turned on their heels and stomped out of the room. I followed just in time to find them flattening their bodies and sliding under the front door. They stayed away for the next few nights but when they came back again, things got ugly.

*

It had been a tough day at work and I collapsed into bed at half past ten. I had a dream I was being hung. I stood on the gallows and the floor fell away underneath me, dropping me sharply into emptiness. The noose was tight against my neck. I gasped for air and could get none. The rope was cutting into my skin. Then I found myself twisting on the bed, coming to from the dream. Two muddlers were standing on my chest. They were pulling on the cable of my phone charger - wound tight around my throat. Now I was wide awake and I couldn't see the muddlers. But the cord around my throat was real enough, pulled by invisible hands. I forced my fingers under the wire to relieve the pressure. Then, all of a sudden, it went slack. I tried to stand up and pitched onto the floor. My ankles were tied together with shoelaces.

How many muddlers were there? What were they doing now? I tried my breathing trick but the adrenaline was pumping too fast around my system. Now there was a pillow on my face and tiny hands were pressing it down over my nose and mouth. I fought hard to get the pillow off me - muddlers are preternaturally strong. I sprawled onto my belly and scuttered out of the room, pulling the door firmly shut behind me. A vase flew at my head. I arched my body sideways, and the vase hit the wall and smashed into pieces. I scanned the room, looking for the next projectile. I should have looked behind me. Something came down hard on the back of my skull. The room spun and went black.

*

I could hear running water and I was shivering. I opened my eyes. Muddlers were standing like squat blue soldiers on parade on the edge of my bath tub, looking down at me. The tub was filling rapidly. The water was almost over my nose. I dragged myself out of the tub, sloshing water in all directions. I staggered into the hallway and ducked, just in time, as a bottle flew at me, then a candlestick. As I reached the front door, there was a heavy *thunk* and a kitchen knife embedded itself in the doorframe. I ran out into the corridor, yelling.

My elderly neighbour, Roona, stuck her head out. 'Goodness, Nick my dear, what on earth's the matter?'

'They're in there!' I said. 'They're trying to kill me.'

'Who are?'

'Them!' I pointed in the direction of my apartment.

'All right, lovey. Why don't you come in? You can't stand here dripping all over the hallway.'

She took me inside, brought me a towel and

poured me a brandy. 'Why don't you tell me what's going on?'

'There are these things. Little things. They're trying to kill me.'

'I see. And why do they want to do that?'

'Because I know about them.'

'Right.'

'They mess around with people. They mess around with all of us. They tangle things up, hide your keys, you know?'

'Okay. And they want to kill you because you found out they hid your keys?'

'I'm the only one that can see them.'

'You probably are, dear.'

'You don't believe me.'

'Why don't I get you a nice cup of cocoa?'

'I can't go back. They'll be waiting for me.'

'I suppose you could always stay here. I've got a spare room. But you must go and talk to someone about all this in the morning, Nick. Someone who can help you, someone professional.'

'Yes, I promise.' I knew I looked like a complete lunatic, but Roona was unflappable.

'Well, that's settled, then. I'll get you something dry to wear.'

She showed me into the spare room and brought me a pink nylon dressing gown. 'This is all I've got I'm afraid. Will it do?'

The dressing gown's frilly cuffs finished an inch above my wrists and I had to grip it tightly at the front to stop it flapping open. I joined Roona in the kitchen and she handed me a steaming mug of cocoa. We chatted for a while. I'd never been inside her flat before. Her husband had died a few years ago and her house had been too big to manage on her own so she'd moved into our block.

'You've done the place up very nicely, Roona.'

'Thank you. My decoration's probably a bit old fashioned for you.'

'No, it's lovely.'

'You're very kind. Now, I expect you'll be wanting to get to bed, what with all the excitement tonight.'

'I'm sorry about that.'

'We all have our moments.'

She ushered me out of the kitchen and said goodnight. I lay down on the bed. Tomorrow I'd go back to my flat. I would feel safer in the daylight. I'd pick up some of my things and ring in sick. Then I'd head to Aunt Aggie's in Aberdeen. She'd be happy to put me up while I figured out what to do.

*

I didn't know what time it was. I was woken up by crashing and screaming in the next room. The place was wrecked, overturned tables and chairs, broken glass, ornaments thrown onto the floor. In the middle of it all, Roona stood with her head in her hands.

'It's them!' I shouted. 'We've got to get out of here.'

I held out my hand to her but a pair of scissors flew past my head and slammed into her chest. Blood spread steadily across her nightgown as she crumpled onto the floor. There was a sudden pounding at the door and everything stopped. Silence.

'Roona? What's going on in there?' More pounding, then the door was kicked open and the two Polish guys from across the hall rushed into the room. They pulled me well away from Roona then one of them examined her. He shook his head. 'She's dead.'

I tried to tell them about the muddlers but it was no use. After that, everything happened very quickly. The police were called and I was taken away. The ruined state of my own apartment only served to confirm people's suspicions. The more I tried to explain what really happened, the madder I seemed. They locked me away along with all the other crazies. Ultimately I was glad. It kept me safe from the muddlers. Maybe I can go home one day when I'm no longer the muddlers' most wanted. Perhaps you think I am mad? Perhaps you think I'm making all of this up? Maybe I'm just 'criminally insane'. That's the phrase. Maybe that's the truth of it. Or maybe, if you learn to meditate, slow your breathing, soften your gaze, you too might see the muddlers.

Go on.

I dare you.

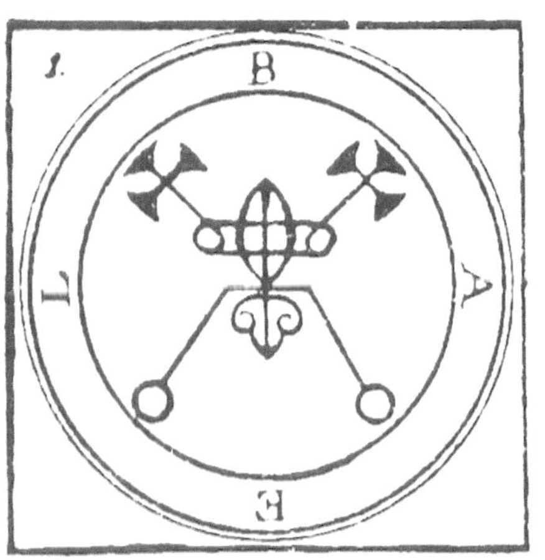

*'He clamped one cuff
around the boy's wrist.'*

POSSESSION

The boy had gone into the garden to escape the noise and heat of the party. He stood by the borders of red and yellow hollyhocks, breathing in their sweet decaying scent. He realised someone was looking at him.

'What are you doing out here all by yourself?' the man asked.

The boy had seen him earlier, standing alone. Watching. 'It was getting stuffy in there.'

For the first time he really looked at the man. He must have been in his late thirties. He was stocky and handsome in spite of his pockmarked face.

'How do you know Jacob?' the boy asked.

'Who's Jacob?'

'The guy giving the party.'

'I don't know him. How old are you?'

'Nineteen.'

'Good.'

'What's good about it?'

'I like young guys.'

The boy felt the heat rising in him. He fidgeted and looked down at the ground, wanting the man to move closer.

'My car's outside. D'you want to go?' the man said.

*

He had an old black Subaru with a spoiler on the back. They drove out of the city onto the motorway. It was early morning and the lanes were empty. The boy enjoyed watching the man shifting gears, his leg muscles flexing as he rode the clutch, driving fast. The boy didn't care where they were going. Eventually they pulled off onto an unlit lane. They stopped at a crumbling old cottage. It had a thatched roof and there were cracked panes of glass in its latticework windows. The paint on its walls was fading. The boy could see the lights of the motorway in the distance.

In the kitchen, four stick-back chairs were placed around a pine table. A bare bulb hung from the ceiling giving the room a cold, stark brightness. An old freestanding fridge droned in the corner as the man filled the kettle.

'Coffee?' he said.

'Sure. Do you live here alone?'

'Yeah.'

'It's nice.'

'It needs some work doing.'

'Are you handy, then?'

'Yeah. I just haven't had the time.'

'What do you do?'

'This and that.'

The man seized the boy and kissed him, firm hands on the boy's back. His fingers eased under the waistband of the boy's jeans, pressing against his nakedness beneath. He kneaded the boy's skin with forceful strokes, fingers reaching further down, hitching the boy into him as he kissed his shoulder. The boy heard the gurgling of the kettle, then abruptly it clicked off.

'Let's go to bed,' the man said.

The boy followed without a word. The man sat him down on the bed. He carefully stripped the boy then pushed him onto his back. He took off his own clothes and stood tumescent in front of him. Then he was on him, kissing and stroking and taking what he wanted. When he was done he lifted a towel from the floor and offered it to the boy.

He put his arm around the boy's slim waist, bringing him in to his strong chest. The boy felt like he was wrapped in a warm blanket.

'I want you here,' the man told him, 'but we do things my way.'

The boy liked the way that sounded.

'I need to get some sleep,' the man said. 'I have to

go somewhere in the morning'

'Where?'

'Don't ask questions. There's something I have to do for someone. You'll stay here and wait for me.'

The man held the boy tight against him and they drifted into the oblivion of sleep.

*

The next morning, the boy got up while the man was still sleeping. He watched him for a while then went and checked the kitchen cupboards. He heard the man in the shower as he made toast and coffee. The man had changed into a blue Henley shirt and faded Levis. The boy liked the way he looked. Sitting down at the table, the man put on a pair of scuffed trainers and bit into a slice of toast.

'Eat up. I have to go soon,' he said

The boy watched the way the man took big mouthfuls of cereal and swigs of coffee. The man gripped the boy's thigh.

'Time for me to go. Come on.'

They went back into the bedroom and the man pushed the boy down on the bed again. He held the boy fast, pushing one knee into his chest, restricting his breathing. The boy moaned. The man took hold of one of his wrists. He produced a pair of handcuffs. He clamped one cuff around the boy's wrist and the other around one of the rods of the bedstead. The boy struggled and kicked but the man was too strong.

'Stop moving about,' the man told him.

'Please, don't do this. I promise I won't go anywhere.'

'It's just to make sure.'

'I don't want to be chained up.'

'It won't be for long. And it won't be forever. Only until I can trust you. I don't want you going outside without my permission.'

The boy's heart was thundering. His breath coming quick and fast.

'I'll be back soon.'

'Please don't leave me like this.'

The man ignored him. He went to a drawer, pulled out a gun and checked it was loaded.

'What's that for?' The boy's voice croaked and his chest hurt.

'It's not your concern.'

The man kissed him, stroking the gun against the boy's cheek before putting it in his back pocket. When the man was gone, the boy lay still on the bed and his heart began to slow. He stared up at the ceiling and its fish-scale plasterwork, and began counting every groove and curve. He was tired from the night before and soon fell asleep.

*

His handcuffed arm, stretched up above his head, was tingling. He didn't know how long he'd slept but the sunlight flooding the room had turned golden. He sat up and tugged at the bedstead. It gave just a little. With his free hand, he began to twist it from side to side then up and down. If he could just twist it free, he might be able to slide the handcuffs over the top. He pressed his shoulder against the wood and pushed as hard as he could. The beam started to give. He pushed harder and he was free.

He opened the bedside drawers and poked around inside. The key wasn't there. The man must have taken it with him. It didn't matter. He'd get help with the cuffs later.

He tried the front and the back door. Both were locked. All the windows were locked too. There was a large sash window in the living room big enough to climb through but there was no key for the lock. The boy searched around the room. Eventually, he found the key in a wooden trinket box by the fireplace. The window was stiff from lack of use. He squared himself against the casing and heaved. The wood groaned and the window cracked open.

A wide, desiccated potato field stood between the house and the roaring motorway. Once he reached the motorway he could flag someone down. About a hundred yards away was a break in the hedgerow. He climbed through it into the field. The ground was dry and dusty underfoot.

He hurried across the uneven trenches of the potato field. He stumbled and pitched forwards onto the thirsty earth. Dust covered his jeans and tee shirt and made him cough. He lay still for a moment. He thought about being with the man the night before, how sure it felt. He hadn't understood then what the man really wanted. He looked towards the motorway and saw the man's black sports car coming down the slip road. It turned onto the lane leading to the cottage. If the boy moved quickly he could just get back to the cottage in time. If he did, the man would make sure he never escaped again. Or he could continue across the field to freedom. He imagined the man's brutal, punishing hands on his body. The man's breath, hot against his neck as he forced himself inside, invading him.

The boy stood up, the muscles tightening in his jaw as his eyes darted between the cottage and the motorway. Brushing the dirt from his clothes, he started to run.

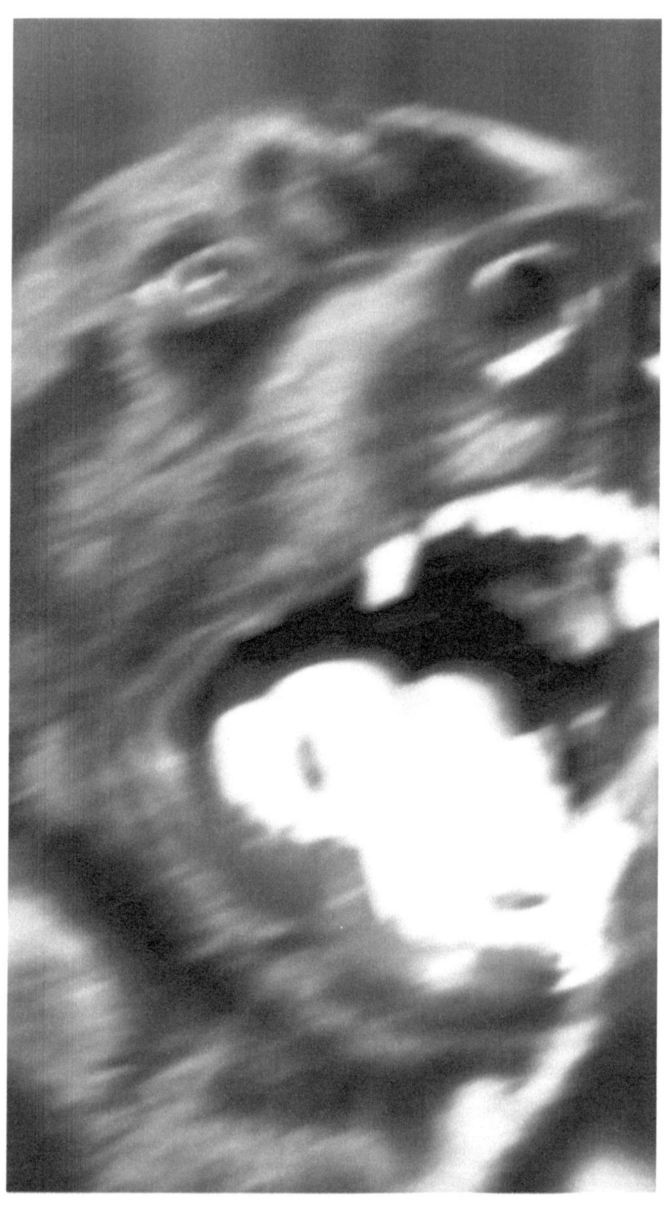

*'Its howling makes its victim's blood run
cold but its footfalls make no sound.'*

BLACK SHUCK

A cooling breeze murmured through the ancient yew trees. The moss-grown faces of gargoyles faded in the darkling churchyard. Two teenage boys made their way towards the abandoned church, which stood watch mournfully over the sleeping dead. They dropped their rucksacks and sat down, resting their backs against crumbling headstones. Kenny scrolled on his phone, his face wraith-like in its glow, thumbs dancing rhythmically. 'Hey Vijay, listen to this,' he said. 'Black Shuck, the hound of hell, has terrorised Norfolk and Suffolk for centuries. It takes the form of a huge black dog, prowling along dark lanes and lonely footpaths. Its howling makes its victim's blood run cold but its footfalls make no sound. In 1957, a newspaper reported the narrow escape of a man cycling home one winter night. An enormous black dog appeared on the road behind him. He pedalled furiously but the monstrous animal, jaws slobbering, was almost upon him. Suddenly a car came from the other direction and the creature disappeared into the night.' Kenny paused for effect. 'An encounter with Black Shuck brings certain calamity. See the beast and you will surely die.'

'What a load of bullshit,' Vijay said.

'Of course it is, mate. But we can scare the girls with it when they get here, make them cosy up.'

'Have you ever seen Leah Jameson scared of anything?'

'Maybe not. But there's always a first time. Summer's way hotter than Leah anyway, with all that long blonde hair and big tits.'

'I'm more of a leg man. But Leah ain't a bad looking piece.'

'You can have her.'

'What d'you reckon to our chances of getting off with them?'

'Pretty good. With enough drink.' Kenny unzipped his backpack and pulled out a bottle of sweetish Plymouth Gin.

'That is so fucking gay, man. It's an old lady's drink,' Vijay said.

'It was all I could find. It was right at the back of the drinks cabinet - so mum won't miss it.'

'Give it here.' Vijay unscrewed the lid and took a

swig, then coughed and grimaced. 'It tastes like cough syrup.'

'You won't notice after a while.' Kenny snatched the bottle and took a couple of glugs. He let out a hollow belch. Both boys snickered.

'Isn't it weird how Leah and Summer are always hanging around together?' Vijay said. 'Like Siamese twins.'

Kenny adopted a man-of-the-world tone. 'Girls are like that, mate. They even go to the frigging toilet together.'

'Why do they do that?'

'Who knows? Who cares? I just want to get my hands on Summer Mallory's knockers.'

'You randy bastard,' Vijay nodded towards the bottle 'Give me some more of that.'

'I thought it was gay and tasted like cough medicine?'

'It's not so bad. Babycham - now that's really gay.'

'Prosecco's gay.'

'Pina Colada's gay.'

'Tia Maria's gay.'

The boys fell about, laughing. Vijay's face became serious as he swigged more gin.

'Do you think anyone missed us when we snuck out?'

'Probably,' Kenny said. 'But, so what? Everyone messes about on school trips. It's tradition. Are you having second thoughts? Going to piss your panties and run on back to Miss Thomas?'

'No.'

'You're such a nancy boy sometimes.'

'Shut up, Kenny.'

'Where are those stupid girls? I reckon we've got a good chance of getting to second base tonight.'

'I dunno, Ken. I can't believe Leah would -'

Something malevolent, guttural, sounded clearly in the distance.

'Whoa, what the fuck was that?' Vijay's voice rose as he spoke.

'Dunno.' Kenny peered around the graveyard. A dull grey mist was snaking its way between the headstones. It was getting darker now. Kenny unzipped the front pocket of his rucksack and pulled out a flick-knife.

'What did you bring that for?' Vijay asked.

'Protection. In case there were any crazies knocking around.'

'In a churchyard, in the middle of nowhere?'

'I'm not taking any chances, mate. That photographer bloke got drained of blood in a graveyard. It was all over the news.'

Kenny nudged Vijay in the stomach.

'Come on. Let's go and see what that noise was.'

'I'm not so sure, man. What if it's a rabid dog?'

'There's no rabies in England, dickhead,' Kenny said.

'I still don't like it.'

'Why are you such a gay boy? It's probably just a fox. We can hunt it.'

'It didn't sound like a fox. It sounded like…'

'Black Shuck?' Vijay didn't like the way Kenny sniggered.

'I don't think you can just go around killing foxes, mate. There's laws.'

'Watch me.'

*

The day was almost dead. The spectral mist gave way to shadowy woodland. Twisted branches formed an arch into the blackness beyond.

'I don't fancy this, Ken,' Vijay said.

Kenny tapped the torch app on his phone and disappeared into the wood. If only they'd stayed in the dorm at the education centre. Coming out here was a dumb idea. All because Kenny thought they could scare two birds into making out. Vijay didn't really fancy Leah or Summer that much anyway. He was more interested in Priyanka from the year below.

'Kenny?' Where the hell was he? 'Kenny, you dick. Stop arsing about.'

Nothing.

Vijay felt his balls shrivel. The primal urges of fight or flight battled inside him. Flight was winning.

'Come on, man. Leah and Summer might have turned up by now.'

Vijay heard a violent snapping of branches. Something was coming towards him - and fast. His breath failed in his chest. He backed away just as Kenny stumbled through the trees, almost knocking him over.

'Run! Get out of here!' he yelled. 'It's coming.'

A huge black dog leapt out of the shadows. Its fiery eyes shone in the dark. They watched as the creature paced from side to side, choosing its moment. It gave a long, sonorous growl as it tensed its powerful frame, then it sprang, mouth wide, flecks of yellow drool spinning into the air. It smacked into Kenny, throwing him onto his back. He fought desperately with the beast, its jaws snapping inches from his face. Then it buried its teeth into his neck, ripping the flesh away. His cries became more anguished, then suddenly he stopped screaming altogether. Vijay tried to run but his legs wouldn't oblige. The animal raised its head. Kenny's blood dripped from its jaws as it moved towards him. He gave a single high-pitched scream and the air rang hollow with its echo.

*

'Are you sure this is the right place?' Summer asked dubiously.

'Yeah,' Leah said. 'This is definitely it. Though God knows where those two doofuses are.'

She pushed the dilapidated gate open and walked into the gloomy churchyard. Summer followed, pulling her jacket closer around her shoulders.

'Hey look,' Leah said, 'those are their bags.'

'Then where are they?'

'No idea. Let's see if they've left any drink behind.' She rifled through Kenny's rucksack. 'Tah-dah!' The gin bottle glinted as she held it up in the moonlight.

'I don't like this, Leah,' Summer said. 'Where have they got to?'

'It's probably just some dumb prank they're playing. Think they're gonna scare us.' Leah patted the ground beside her and Summer sat down. Leah kissed her. Summer let the kiss linger a moment until she broke it.

'What if there's something wrong?' Summer said.

'There isn't.'

Leah's lips, soft and eager, moved down Summer's neck. Summer arched her neck, inviting her to go deeper.

'All the same,' she said, 'I think we should at least try and find out where they are.'

Leah looked up. 'You're killing the mood, honey.'

'Sorry.'

She began to unbutton Summer's shirt, easing her onto her back. Summer ran her fingers through Leah's rich auburn hair, pushing aside the curls as they fell over her face. They kissed each other feverishly. Leah teased Summer's nipple with her thumb and spiralled her fingers down over her midriff. Her skin was like pale sunrise. Then the sound came, raw and predatory, cutting through the air.

'Jesus, what was that?' Summer sat up.

'I dunno. Just the boys pissing around probably.'

'I don't think it is, Leah.'

'Come on, darling. Relax. Enjoy the moment.'

'That was some kind of animal. Something's out there.' Summer began to button up her shirt as she stood up.

Leah sighed. 'Okay, we'll go and take a look. But, I'm telling you, that's exactly what Kenny and his sidekick want us to…'

Leah's words tailed off as Summer pointed to the middle distance, one hand over her mouth. Just beyond the edge of the mist, Black Shuck was looking at them.

'Shit. Run!' Leah said.

They ran towards the abandoned church as the beast began to move. Its powerful legs propelled it forwards with uncanny speed. They closed the heavy oak door just as the animal smashed into it with its massive bulk. Black Shuck hurled itself against the door again and again. The door juddered on its hinges. The latch rattled loosely in its rusted keep. Leah knew it wouldn't hold for long. She pulled Summer down into the pews before the door smashed open. The beast's heavy steps moved down the central aisle of the nave towards the chancel. The animal was only feet away from them. Leah noticed the steps leading up to the bell tower. She signalled to Summer to stay down and stay quiet.

'Hey, Fido!' she shouted. The creature spun round. 'Come and get me.'

She sprinted for the stairs. The dog leapt across the pews. Its claws scraped on the stone floor. Leah had almost made it when the dog struck her in the back with juggernaut force. The breath was knocked out of her. Black Shuck was on top of her, its incredible weight pinning her to the floor. She waited for the kill. There was a beat, a hesitation, then she felt its warm breath and its head nudging her face. It licked her gently. She heard Summer's footsteps on the flagstones then Summer hugged the giant animal. Leah looked at the huge black dog properly for the first time. Its shining eyes were wild, feral and, at the same time, beautiful. 'I don't believe it.'

'She didn't attack you.'

'She?'

Summer held her hand out to Leah. 'Yes, *she*! Now... you were in the middle of taking my shirt off...'

They wandered back to the churchyard, arm in arm, and Black Shuck trotted contentedly behind them through the last of the clearing mist.

'His hair was fuller and swept back from his
forehead. His shoulders were broader.'

NEW, IMPROVED

Wipers swiped at the rain lashing the windscreen. As the car battled along the muddy track it was all Cam could do to keep from sliding into a ditch. Up ahead he was just able to make out a solitary white house at the edge of the woods. It had been a long drive and he was pleased it was over as he pulled up in front of the heavy oak door. The door opened.

'Cam. How are you? How was the drive? It's so great to see you.'

'It's great to see you too, Liam. Boy, you've changed. I hardly recognised you.'

'It's been over a year.'

'Even so.'

Liam's usually lifeless hair was fuller and swept back from his forehead. His once skinny arms showed impressive guns. His birdlike legs had thickened into tree trunks. His shoulders were broader, eyes greener, nose more delicate and a carpet of designer stubble swept across his chin.

'Come in out of the cold and rain.' He showed Cam into the living room and brought in a couple of Nastro Azzurros.

'I still can't believe how much you've altered,' Cam said. 'This new man of yours must be good for you.'

'I'm very happy,' Liam replied. 'It's being away from London too. Londoners are obsessed with how much people earn, how well everyone is doing. It's different here. I feel more alive.'

'You certainly look it.'

'I jog every morning, spend a couple of hours at the gym.'

Cam remembered how much Liam used to hate exercise. When they shared a flat together, he rarely got out of bed before noon at the weekend. 'What does your new man do?'

'He's a scientist.'

Probably a plastic surgeon, Cam thought, and a damn good one.

Liam drank some more beer. 'Are you still with Donny, Cam?'

'Afraid so.'

'I thought you two were made for each other.'

'I'm just joking. He's still cute, if a little gone to seed.' Cam was only half-joking. He and Donny had been drifting apart for several months now. That was partly why Cam had decided to look up his old flatmate. He needed to get away. Donny could certainly take some notes from the new, improved Liam.

'Sounds like all he needs is a fitness programme,' Liam said. 'Once you get started, it's fairly easy to maintain, especially if you have an addictive personality.'

'I'll take your word for it.'

A car pulled up outside and Liam leapt up. 'It's him!' He hurried outside.

Cam saw a hunched little man get out of a black BMW. Liam brought him in. 'This is Oscar!' Oscar extended a bony hand. Wispy hair crowned a high forehead and his eyes were underlined by dark shadows. Cam reckoned he must be at least twenty years older than Liam.

'Pleased to meet you,' Cam said.

Oscar's soulless stare cut through him. 'I hope Liam has been looking after you. I apologise I was not here to greet you on your arrival. I had some urgent business at the laboratory.'

'What field of research are you in?'

Oscar wagged a finger. 'It's not really research, as you'd understand the term. It's more the development of new scientific frontiers.'

'My clever man works so hard,' said Liam, massaging Oscar's shoulders. 'What can I get you darling?'

'A scotch and soda, thank you.'

Liam disappeared into the kitchen. Cam had never seen him so eager to please.

'You have known Liam a long time, I think?' Oscar said.

'We used to share a flat together in Leytonstone but I haven't seen him for ages.'

'And here you are.' Oscar's smile was ice.

'He seems to be happy,' Cam said.

'Ours is a simple but pleasant existence.'

'Yes,' Liam added as he brought Oscar his drink. 'Walks in the forest, candlelit suppers, movies and a good bottle of wine.' He touched the back of Oscar's head gently. He never used to be so affectionate.

'And where did you two meet?' Cam directed his question at Liam but it was Oscar who answered.

'He was temping at Reading University and I was giving a lecture there. He was tasked with looking after me for the day.'

'And I haven't stopped since.'

'So, are you a full-time houseboy now?' Cam asked.

'I love taking care of the house.'

Cam couldn't hide his surprise. Liam had always been one of the messiest people he knew. He left piles of dirty dishes in the sink and had to be badgered into cleaning the flat. 'You're certainly transformed. It must be the country air.'

Oscar changed the subject. 'Are we having the venison stew tonight?'

'Yes, it's all cooking nicely,' Liam said.

'I'm sure you'll enjoy it Cameron. Liam's stews are always excellent.'

Liam went to check on the food. Cam broke the awkward silence.'You and Liam seem to be very much in love.'

'We are.'

'The perfect couple even.'

'Possibly.'

'I'm quite amazed at the change. Liam seems such a different person to the one I used to know.'

'People change.' Oscar eyed Cam darkly. 'Tell me about you.'

'There's not much to tell,' Cam said. 'I work as a freelance journalist. I've been seeing the same guy for the past three years.'

'Why is he not here with you?'

'He'd be bored listening to Liam and me go on about the good old days.'

'And are you and your partner happy?'

'We're doing all right. He isn't quite the buff and well-trained homemaker Liam is, though.'

'You sound disappointed.'

'Maybe I am.'

Liam came back and Oscar suggested he gave Cam a tour of the house. Cam was glad to get away. Oscar gave him the creeps.

The house had an almost space-age feel. Cubist art hung against glossy white walls. A James Seccombe plastic bed dominated the master bedroom. Even so, the atmosphere was stark rather than playful. There was one room in the house that Liam was careful to avoid: Oscar's study in the basement.

The venison stew was delicious and Oscar chose a Château Palmer Margaux to go with it. As Liam cleared the plates, Oscar refilled their glasses.

'You said earlier you were developing new technological frontiers, Oscar,' Cam said. 'What frontiers, exactly?'

'Some of my work is of a very delicate nature. I'm exploring new ways to treat conditions of the dermis and epidermis. I have developed a synthetic tissue that can replace damaged skin. It can be used to treat burns and similar traumas.'

'That's incredible.'

'The work is in its early stages. One interesting development is that the synthetic skin does not age as rapidly as normal skin.'

'I imagine there are people who would kill to get their hands on that.'

'Yes. But, as I say, the work is at an early stage.'

Liam brought coffee cups and petits fours to the table.

'You must be very protective of your work,' Cam said. 'Liam showed me every room in the house except your study.'

'The work I do is groundbreaking. The corporation I work for has concerns about industrial espionage, intellectual property theft, and that sort of thing. That is why my study has to be completely off limits.' Something about Oscar's tone roused Cam's journalistic curiosity.

By the time dinner was over, it was eleven o'clock. Oscar went straight to bed but Liam and Cam stayed up talking. Cam was keen to reminisce but Liam guided the conversation in other directions. He questioned Cam again about Donny, their relationship, old friends, his job. It was past 1am when they said goodnight.

Cam waited half an hour then got out of bed and crept into the hallway. He was greeted by shadow and silence. He stole through the house to the basement, took out a metal toothpick, and set to work on the study door. He hadn't broken into anywhere since his exposé of dodgy health farms. It was a couple of minutes before the lock clicked open. He hadn't lost the knack. He eased the door shut behind him and turned on the light. Tall metal cabinets stood along the walls. In the centre of the room was what looked like an operating table.

Cam tried each cabinet in turn but they were all locked. There was a desk in the far corner piled high with papers: diagrams, schematics, notes on human anatomy. He pulled open a drawer. Inside was what appeared to be a death mask of Liam's face. Cam spun round. The door had opened. Oscar and Liam came in.

'You shouldn't be in here.' Cam could hear the anger rising in Oscar's voice.

Cam held up the death mask. 'What's this for?

'It's nothing for you to be concerned about, Cam. Give me the mask,' Liam said.

Liam held out his hand and Cam found himself handing the mask over.

'Has Oscar been experimenting on you, Liam? Is that why you're so different?' Liam punched Cam smartly in the gut. Next Cam felt a sharp blow to the back of his neck, then Liam seized his throat and crushed it between his fingers. Cam kneed Liam hard in the groin but it had no effect. He thrust the tooth pick into Liam's arm. No blood. He pushed the point up into Liam's eye. Liam released his grip and Cam dragged himself free, sucking in precious mouthfuls of air. Liam stumbled around, arms windmilling. He crashed into a metal cabinet, then sprawled over the operating table. Then he was still.

Cam stood up on shaky legs as Oscar produced a gun from his desk. 'You interfering idiot!' he shouted.

'What have you done with Liam? The real Liam?'

'Let's just say I decommissioned him. Then I made this replica in his image, with certain enhancements.'

Cam kicked out at him, catching him on the wrist. The gun clattered to the floor. Cam tackled Oscar to the ground and held him down. He wasn't sure why, but suddenly he thought about Donny. How faded he was, how routine their relationship had become.

'We needn't be enemies, Oscar. What you've done

here is genius. Maybe we could be of use to each other. You'll need a new guinea pig. I'm with a guy who could do with some… improvements.'

Oscar looked at him squarely. 'Well now, exactly what did you have in mind?'

'Unruly black hair tumbled down onto
the intruder's broad shoulders.'

PROWLER

Mason Grimes escaped from Blackmoor Maximum Security Prison late last night and a manhunt across Dorset and Hampshire has so far failed to apprehend him. Grimes is an extremely dangerous and violent criminal and the public are advised that he should not be approached under any circumstances…

Greg switched off the radio. He checked the back door was locked, turned on the outside light and peered out. Shadows slithered across the brickwork, the wind buffeted the plants in the courtyard. He looked at the bottle of wine on the kitchen counter. Plenty left still. He emptied the contents into his glass, and necked it. Then he checked his watch: 9.13pm. He selected Marshall's number on his mobile. Marshall answered after two rings. 'Hey.'

Marshall's voice was hollow over the speakerphone.

'Where are you, Marshall?'

'The meeting ran late.'

'You're telling me.'

'There was nothing I could do.'

'You're dinner's in the dog. If we had a dog.'

'I'm almost there. I'm literally turning onto our road now.'

Greg drained and rinsed his glass. By the time Marshall was home, the glass was neatly put away.

Greg steadied himself against the worktop and waited for the games to begin. 'How much have you had to drink? Marshall asked.

'A glass at lunchtime.'

'You're a bad liar.'

'So are you.'

'What's that supposed to mean?'

'Where have you really been tonight, Marshall? Out with the office junior?'

'Fuck off, Greg.'

'You're a real charmer.'

'I told you, I was in a meeting. It ran on. I don't have to explain myself to a drunk.'

'I'm not drunk.'

'Your face is flushed and you're talking too loudly. Sober up and go to bed.'

Greg had been anxious all day. A drink had helped. He followed Marshall into the sitting room.

'Did you hear? There's a maniac on the loose.'

'No I didn't.'

'It's all over the news.'

'I've been busy.'

Greg felt giddy. He knew he wasn't in any condition for a fight. 'You know, you're right. I think I will go to bed.'

'I'll be up later.'

'There's some shepherd's pie in the fridge. You can warm it up, if you're hungry.'

*

Greg sat on the bed and let out a deep sigh. He was baking hot. His fingertips were tingling. He fetched a glass of water and checked himself over in the bathroom mirror. A few more wrinkles but his looks hadn't gone entirely to pot yet. Marshall's voice drifted up from below. He was probably on the phone to the spotty office boy. Greg imagined the two of them: the kid dressed up in skintight school uniform, begging to be disciplined; Marshall slavering over him in pervy schoolmaster's get up. Greg began to chuckle. He felt floaty. He must have nodded off. The next thing he knew, Marshall was standing in front of him, belly seeping over the waistband of his boxers.

'You need to get undressed.'

'What time is it?' Greg said muzzily.

'11.45.'

'I must have passed out.'

'Drunks usually do.'

'At least I didn't have to listen to you sweet talking

the infant you've been shafting.'

Marshall shook his head and walked off. Greg heard him brushing his teeth. Greg stripped and slipped naked between the covers, savouring the coolness of the sheets against his skin. When Marshall climbed in beside him, he pretended to be asleep. In a couple of minutes Marshall was snoring heavily. Greg began to feel less groggy. He was awake now and lay in the darkness for what seemed like an age. He checked his watch again: 12.33. Then he heard footsteps coming from downstairs.

'Marshall!'

The snoring continued. Greg gave him a sharp prod.

'Marshall. Wake up.'

Marshall stared dumbly at Greg, bleary-eyed. 'What?'

'Wake up, Marshall. There's someone in the house.'

'You're still pissed. Go back to sleep.'

'There's someone down there.'

'And I'm telling you to go to sleep.'

'Please Marshall, I heard something.'

Marshall swung his legs over the side of the bed and sat up. 'If this is another drunken hallucination…'

'Someone's in the house.'

'For God's sake.'

'Perhaps it's that escaped nutcase.'

'There's only one nutcase in this fucking house.'

'What are we going to do?'

'Shhh.' Marshall tilted his head. 'I don't hear anything.'

'I can't go back to sleep, Marshall. I'm too scared.'

'Jesus Christ. You are bloody priceless.'

'I'm going to phone the police.'

'Don't be ridiculous. I'll go and take a look.'

Greg heard him thumping down the stairs, then banging doors as he moved from room to room. Then the house was silent. Still silent. Greg went outside and leaned over the banister.

'Marshall? Are you okay?' No response. His heart was beating fast against the cage-work of his ribs. Slowly, he made his way downstairs. Marshall's body lay twisted on the carpet, head tilted oddly, eyes gawking, blood pumping slowly from a wound in his head. A man, obscured by a black ski mask, was standing over him. The man advanced purposefully and swiftly towards Greg. Greg ripped the mask off and unruly black hair tumbled down onto the man's broad shoulders. The man seized Greg and kissed him powerfully on the lips. After a few seconds, Greg pulled away.

'Why didn't you say something when I called out?'

'I dunno, baby. I guess I wasn't thinking. I've never killed a guy before.'

'He's definitely dead?'

The man nodded. 'Definitely.'

Greg went over to Marshall's body and prodded

at it with his toe.

'Well done. Did you come in through the back door?'

'Everything exactly as we said. The lock's busted. Looks like a professional job.'

'We need to mess the place up to make the robbery story work.'

They ransacked the room in methodical silence.

'Now I'd better call the police.'

'I need a stiff drink before I go, baby.'

'You shouldn't, Jack. Time is getting on.'

'Come on, Greg. I've just committed murder.'

'I suppose we should mark the occasion.'

'Put some clothes on too. Not that I'm complaining.'

Greg took his time pouring two vodkas. He liked the thought of Jack savouring his nakedness. He handed over a glass. 'Here's to a brighter and richer future.'

Jack drank fast then wiped his lips with the back of a gloved hand.

Greg winked. 'Okay, lover. Off you go. Time for me to play the grieving widow.'

Greg went into the kitchen to wash the glasses. A chill breeze filtered in through the open door. Jack came up behind him, wrapped his arms around his waist and kissed him on the neck. Jack's warmth felt good against him.

'I love you, Greg.'

'I know. But you'd better go now. I've got to put

some clothes on and make that call.'

*

Greg went back to look at Marshall's corpse. Its black eyes reproached him. Greg felt a small stab of dread in the pit of his stomach. He switched on the radio and breezy jazz music drifted through the house. Then he saw Jack's ski mask lying on the floor. His DNA would be all over it. It was the one small mistake that could land them both with a life sentence. Everything hinged on getting rid of it, getting it out of the house now. Jack couldn't have got far. Greg snatched up the mask and ran out into the courtyard - and stumbled over something in the darkness. He was winded for a moment, lying breathless on the ground. He snapped to, realising he had stumbled over Jack's body lying face down, sticky with blood. He lifted Jack's head, stroking back the bloody curls. He stifled a cry. Then someone was at his back, lifting him into the air. A cold blade sliced through the skin of his throat and he felt his own blood warm against his hands. The sound of the radio floated out cheerily into the dark.

The hunt continues for mass murderer Mason Grimes. The public are warned to keep all doors and windows locked. Grimes is a dangerous psychopath and police have advised everyone to remain extremely vigilant…

*'The flimsy wooden window frame had been ripped
out and I could see my breath in the freezing air.'*

THE SWEDISH HOUSE

I pulled my woollen hat tight over my ears and walked across the dimly-lit high school yard. The pavements outside the main gate glittered with ice. The empty Swedish streets suggested a neutron bomb had fallen, or aliens had landed, or a pandemic had struck. Tonight's lesson had not gone well. I had totally misjudged the students' abilities. Their English was too advanced for the material I had prepared and they devoured the exercises like so many hungry wolves. There was still half an hour to go and I was struggling to think of something to fill the time. They watched me in sombre Nordic silence until a whiskered oddball suggested a conversation about hobbies. He delivered a heavily accented monologue on catching and killing and gutting fish, turning me, and the rest of the class, green at the gills.

I was determined to be better prepared next time. If any of them came back. Perhaps I wasn't cut out to be an English teacher after all. I'd seen it as my passport to Europe. Just after I'd accepted this job, I was offered a much better one in Munich. Back then I hadn't realised EFL contracts aren't worth the paper they're written on. I had been overly conscientious and now I was stuck in a faceless town, surrounded by frozen pine forests and black, bottomless lakes.

The lights of the little high street retreated behind me as I walked up the hill. The rundown old house I called home was perched halfway up a muddy track with the melodic name, Ålandsvägen. It was where my landlady, Solveig Gunnarson had grown up. Her father had died in a boating accident just after she was born. Two years ago, her mother had also died. Inside the old house, the mother's presence was everywhere. Outworn furniture, chipped floral crockery, a cast-iron mangle - all reminded me it was her house, not mine. It was as if the house resented me. The antiquated oven had no thermostat and my meals were either burned black or lukewarm. The shower ran cold suddenly for no reason and the bed made my back ache. Every room smelled stale and dead. Like all old buildings, the house made unsettling sounds in the night. More than once I found an ornament smashed, as if someone had thrown it in silent rage.

Towering over the house was the five-bedroomed new build Solveig had built with her husband, Staffan. A third property - a bungalow - was hunched at the bottom of the track. Solveig said people lived there but I never saw anyone. The three buildings stood like ill-matched sentinels, just off the main route out of Uddevalla. They comprised a parochial town's last sentry post before the E6 wound its way south through Bohuslän's vast forest towards Gothenburg. I wondered for the thousandth time what on earth I was doing here. I had no friends, no boyfriend, no life to speak of. Just lonely weekends checking mousetraps and watching English football - or *Dallas* with Swedish subtitles. I didn't even like football or *Dallas*, but there was nothing else to do except wander around in the merciless cold, window-shopping for things I couldn't afford.

I trudged along Ålandsvägen. I saw Solveig and Staffan's lights were on which brightened my mood a bit. As always, I struggled with the lock on my front door. The windowless hallway was unusually bright. Normally, I kept the bathroom door closed to conserve heat but now it was thrown wide open. A phone directory had been used as a door stop. I crept into the kitchen and flicked on the lights. Everything was as I left it. I checked the living room. Nothing out of place. Then I went into the bedroom. The flimsy window frame had been ripped out and

I could see my breath in the freezing air, and the bedroom had been turned upside down.

Solveig appeared as soon as I rang her doorbell.

'Harry? Is anything the matter?'

'I've been broken into.'

'You have broken something?'

'No, I've been robbed, burgled. Someone came into the house while I was out.'

She called Staffan. He fetched nails and some wood to patch up the window.

Solveig scooped up handfuls of my clothes from the floor of my vandalised bedroom - shirts, sweaters, underpants. I blushed. Staffan boarded up the window and muttered something beyond my limited Swedish. Solveig translated. 'Staffan thinks the burglar was just getting started when you came back. That is why only this room was messed up.'

'You're probably right.'

'This is my mother's house. Maybe they thought she was still in here, hiding her money under the bed. Is anything important missing?'

'I don't think so.'

'Well, Harry, it is all fixed up now. We will get a new window in a couple of days.'

'Okay. Thank you.'

'Do you want to stay with us tonight?'

'Oh, no. I'm fine,' I lied.

'You are not nervous?'

'No.' Second lie. 'I'm from London. I'm used to things like this.' Lie number three.

'Oh, yes, of course. So we will leave you now, Harry.'

'Yes. Thank you for everything.'

'It is not a problem.'

I locked the front door and grabbed a bottle of starköl to steady my jangled nerves. I felt vulnerable and alone. I could simply pack my bags and go home but I didn't like the idea of admitting defeat. My contract ended in July. I'd stick it out till then. The nights would be shorter and lighter, the days illuminated by summer. I could bear to stay on if only the language institute would transfer me to Stockholm where there were plenty of bars and clubs and available Vikings. But the big city jobs were sought after. Little chance for a greenhorn like me. Best just to leave at the end of July. I might even make it to Munich after all.

Warmed by the beer, my stomach told me it was time for dinner.

Then I heard it. A scuffling sound from the floor above. I lived entirely on the ground floor of the house and hadn't thought to look upstairs. The attic room was full of Solveig's mother's things. I went up there when I first moved in and rummaged around out of curiosity but there was something baleful about that room: dusty ornaments, a basket of needlepoint, pictures of dead people. Solveig's mother appeared in a yellowing photo, her face fixed and stern. I'd almost expected her to be standing behind me when I turned to leave.

The sound came again. I held my breath and listened. Somebody was in the house with me. Surely a burglar would have left when I went over to Solveig's. I considered fleeing next door but I didn't want to seem like a milksop in front of Staffan. I'd heard him call me a 'bög', a faggot, under his breath. Best to stay put until morning.

I barricaded myself in the living room, upending an armchair to brace the door. That would at least slow someone down if they tried to force their way in. Fear had dampened the effects of the starköl and I had now cut off my access to any more. I checked the time. Eleven hours to sunrise. I looked up at the low ceiling. I waited, listening for movement from above. But nothing came.

I turned off all the lamps but one and I curled up on the sofa, tucking my hands and feet in for warmth.

*

The front door was shaking in its frame. Someone was trying to get in. Or get out.

Then just as abruptly, it stopped.

I tried to convince myself it was only the wind but I kept seeing Solveig's mother's face, heard her shuffling, imagined her black shawl pulled close around her shoulders, and her face, expressionless as a cadaver.

*

I heard a car pull up outside. I went to the window and peered out through the blinds. There were three men in the car. The driver got out and looked up at the house. I parted the blinds wider for a better look and he must have seen me: he made a show of putting something in the mailbox, got back in the car, and a few seconds later the car was gone. Were they the burglars come back to scope out the house? Or had they come back for their accomplice, still trapped in the attic? I tried to sleep but it was no use. My imagination painted pictures of the intruder on the stairs, scimitar blade raised in the dark.

*

Daylight brought with it a feeling of security. I removed the makeshift barricade and checked upstairs. Of course, there was no one up there. No one but me and the ghostly presence of a long-dead old woman. I showered, dressed and made myself a good breakfast. I checked the mailbox. It was empty. Although I was tired I felt somehow brighter, freer. I knew I couldn't stay here anymore. I would pack my bags tonight, ring my parents and ask them to lend me the air fare back to London. Time to start over. This town was not home and neither was this house. It belonged to a memory.

*

As I left for the last time, I knew she was watching

me from the upstairs window. But it was all right now. I understood.

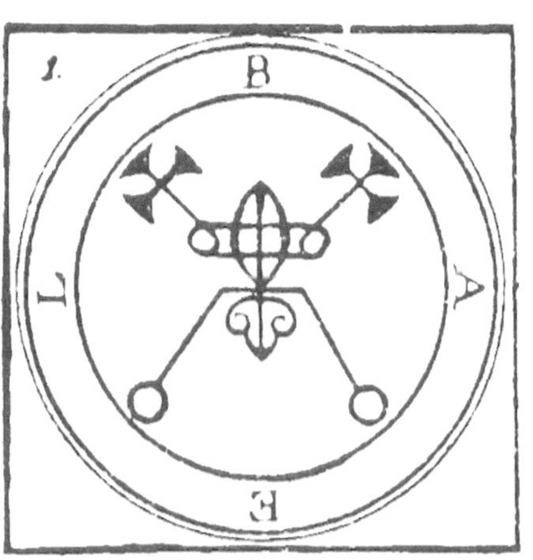

'We have suffered great injustice at the hands of
the Romans but Boudicca has brought us hope.'

ECHOES

The journey from London seemed interminable. Torrential rain meant delays, cancellations and overloaded trains. From Norwich station Patrick took a chugger to Sheringham then the coasthopper bus on to Blakeney. He didn't have time to check in at the hotel before he was due to give his talk. He stood uncertainly at the podium with his battered holdall at his feet. He hated public speaking at the best of times: all those people silently cursing if he overran.

'The Iceni tribe made a treaty with the Romans when Emperor Claudius first invaded Britain in AD 43,' he said. 'They later rebelled in AD 47. After quelling the revolt, the Romans were able to dominate the Iceni through the tribe's more compliant ruler, Prasutagus.'

A man in the audience was staring at him intently.

'When Prasutagus died in AD 61, the Romans tried to annex his kingdom. His widow, Boudicca, was flogged and her daughters raped. At the same time, Roman lenders called in all their loans.'

The man's attention hadn't shifted from Patrick. Patrick wondered if he knew him from somewhere.

'So, while Governor Gaius Paulinus was away fighting a war in Wales, Boudicca led the Iceni and all of East Anglia in a bloody revolt against Roman rule.'

Patrick clicked his remote control and a new slide presented a map of eastern England. He indicated the Roman settlements of Camulodunum and Verulamium which had been involved in the uprising. 'Two cities were ransacked and seventy thousand Romans killed, but the British Isles were now free of Rome. The fact that this disastrous defeat was led by a woman caused the Roman Empire great embarrassment.'

Patrick turned back to the audience. He had one more slide to show: Thomas Thornycroft's statue of Boudicca on the north bank of the Thames. He finished by talking about his plans to write a book on Boudicca and the rise and fall of the Iceni.

Brief applause and then the crowd started filing out of the conference suite.

A few people stayed behind to speak to him. As he fielded their questions, his head began to ache.

He made a show of turning off the projector and packing up his notes. Then he saw the man who had been staring at him so intently. He was with Sir Humphrey Styles, one of the organisers of the East Anglia history conference.

'Patrick, fascinating talk. Can I introduce David Lockhart? He's one of our benefactors from the States. It was his generous donation which enabled us to run the conference.'

The man shook Patrick's hand. He was about the same age as Patrick, handsome with greying temples and soft, searching eyes.

'Then we have a great deal to thank you for, Mr. Lockhart,' Patrick said.

'Call me David. I've always felt a connection to this part of the world. It has a certain mystery and magic to it. I thought your talk was very informative and well-delivered.'

Patrick wanted to stay and talk but his headache was getting worse.

'You want to get up to your room and unwind,' David said, as if reading Patrick's thoughts. 'We mustn't keep you any longer.'

'It was a long, drawn-out journey up from London.'

'Of course. I'm looking forward to your second talk tomorrow.'

Patrick checked in at the desk and headed up to his room. He ordered a sandwich and took a couple of Nurofen. The sandwich turned out to be rather good, but he only managed to eat half of it. He put on Radio Three, stretched out on the bed and soon drifted off to sleep.

*

He was woken up by a soft tapping at the door.

'Who is it?'

'Come on. We have to go.'

He flicked the light switch on but the room remained in darkness. There must have been a power cut. Maybe they were getting everyone out of their rooms for some reason. Fire? Flood?

'Hold on, I'm coming.'

He pulled his clothes on quickly and went to the door. It was David, seeming much younger now in the darkness. He led Patrick down the fire escape and out into the surrounding marshland. Patrick glanced back, expecting to see the hotel's irregular curved profile and mansard roof but there was only open hillside. Blakeney village was gone. Stars glimmered and the brisk night air made everything sharp.

David led the way, arms pistoning as he ran. They were both now shirtless and wore light woollen trousers tied at the waist by woven strips of animal hair. The muddy earth gave way to firmer ground and they found themselves in open flatland. Six wattle and daub roundhouses with thatched straw roofs were arranged around a large fire. A small crowd was listening carefully to a woman with thick, flaming red hair that flowed down to her waist. She wore a large gold necklace and a brightly coloured tunic over which a thick mantle was fastened by a brooch. Her voice boiled with passion and bile. The villagers appeared to recognise David and Patrick as they joined the group and listened.

'These Roman dogs want to steal what is rightfully ours. They do not honour our agreements. My husband left his kingdom to my daughters but the Romans have spurned his legacy. This is why we must rise against them.'

An angry roar rose up from the villagers.

'If you seek a future of prosperity and dignity for our people then we must drive out these heartless invaders. Join us and your courage will stand out as a beacon in the night, calling others to the cause of justice. The spirits of our dead ancestors are with us in our fight. We Iceni shall know no fear in this war of liberation against the enemy. I, Boudicca, call upon you all to take your place alongside me and free our lands forever from these Roman curs.'

The people hollered approvingly, then the chief of the village stepped forward. 'Our Queen has spoken. She will return to her camp this night and we must make ready for war.'

The group stood aside as the chief led Boudicca and her companion away. The two women mounted horses, raised their fists in salute and rode into the darkness. The man quieted the cheering crowd. 'We have suffered great injustice at the hands of the

Romans but Boudicca has brought us hope. Now we have the chance to unite against our oppressors. We shall right the wrongs they have done. This is not just for us, but for our children. They shall claim their birthright as rulers of this land not slaves under the sword of Rome. We must be ready to lay down our lives for that noble cause.'

The drumming of horses hooves sounded in the distance, drawing closer. This was not Boudicca returning, but the sound of many horses. The ominous thundering grew louder and louder and Roman riders charged out of the darkness, attacking the scattering crowd. Men were cut down before they could reach for their weapons. The villagers made for the cover of tall reeds, and David and Patrick did the same, sprinting across open ground with the Romans in close pursuit. Patrick saw a young woman fall in front of a soldier's horse. The soldier struck a downward blow, slashing her with his sword. She gave a choking cry, and then her blood was arcing out of her in warm ribbons.

Patrick and David stumbled blindly through the reeds. The eques scoured the marsh in large numbers. Terrified cries rang out as the villagers were slaughtered with Roman efficiency.

'We're surrounded now,' David whispered.

'What are we going to do?'

'You stay here. I'll lead them away.'

'You'll be killed!'

'No, I can outrun them.'

'Please don't do this, Drust,' Patrick heard himself say.

'I have to, Prasto. Once they take the bait, run for your life.'

'What about you?'

'Don't worry. Wherever you are, I'll find you.'

David stroked Patrick's hair and kissed his lips tenderly, then he turned and vanished through the reeds.

*

Patrick was soaked in sweat and his breathing was very fast. Pale sunlight slipped through a chink in the curtains.

He got dressed and went downstairs.

He was promptly intercepted by Sir Humphrey who insisted on taking him into the lecture room and checking everything was set up properly for his talk. Sir Humphrey was chuffed with the success of the conference and talked at length about the possibilities for a follow-up next year.

By the time Patrick got to the breakfast room, it was almost full and hummed with the chatter of the conference delegates. He found a table by the window, overlooking the little quay and low, flat marshes, and ordered a full English breakfast, and a pot of tea. He was just skimming over his notes when he saw David coming towards him.

'I believe you're giving the first talk this morning.'

'For my sins.'

'I'm very intrigued by your work, Patrick. Particularly the book you're planning on the subject of Boudicca and the Iceni.'

'If I can find the right publisher.'

'It just so happens I own a publishing house. I'd be glad to publish your book.'

'Well, it seems I have another reason to be grateful to you. First you fund this conference and now you're publishing my book.'

'It's a subject close to my heart.' He put his hand on the chair opposite Patrick. 'May I join you?'

'Certainly.'

'You look tired, Patrick. Are you all right?'

'I didn't sleep too well. I had a strange dream.'

'So did I.'

'This may seem an odd question but did it involve Boudicca?'

'Yes, it did,' David said as he leaned forward. 'Didn't I promise you that wherever you are I'd find you?'

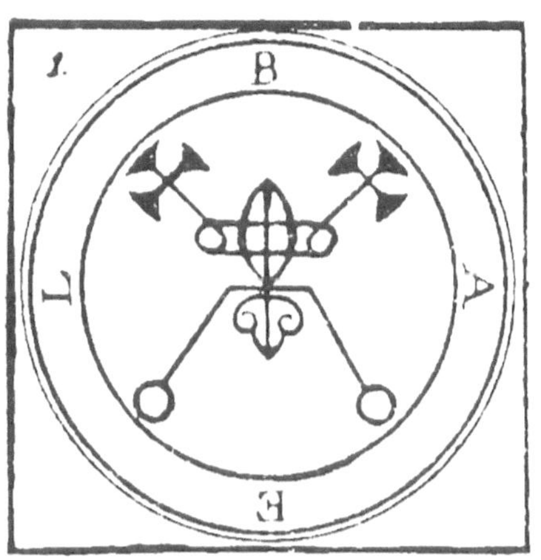

1.
B
A
E
L

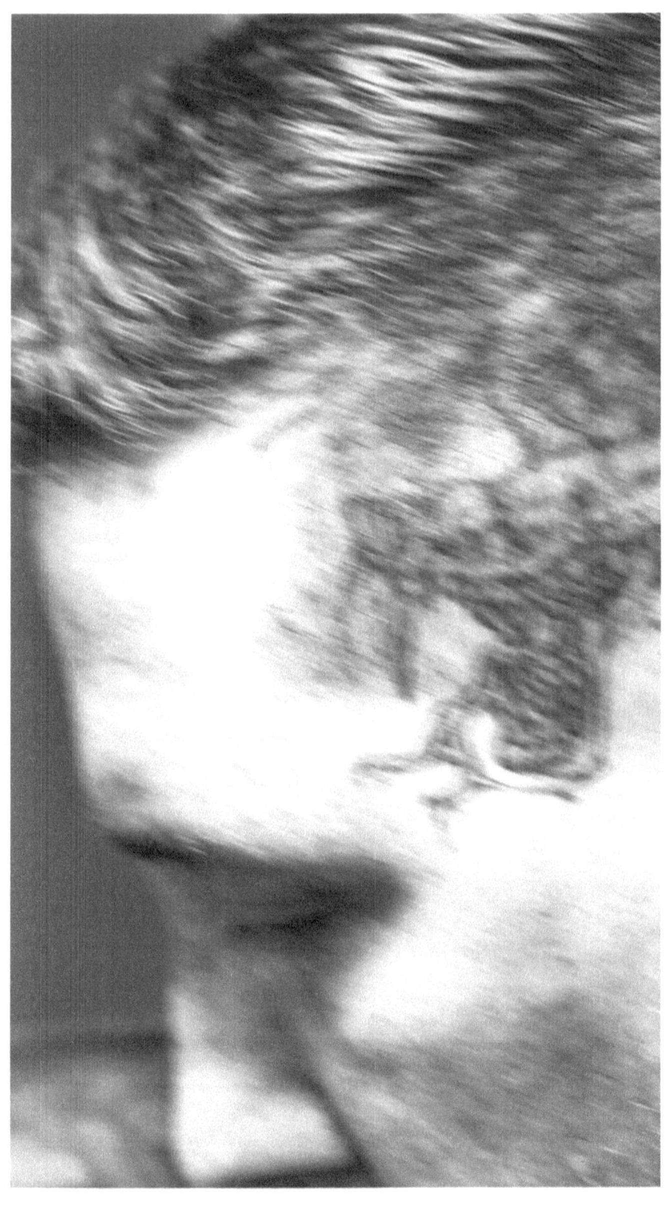

'I live with Charlie.' The guy winked.
'He's out exercising at the moment.'

CHARLIE

The late evening sun cast splashes of light through the trees, speckling the parched earth. Weekday nights were always quiet. No more than five or ten guys out looking for sex. Now only one of them remained. Ricky watched him from his hiding place. The guy was probably in his late forties. He was lean and well groomed, salt-and-pepper hair cut in a flattop. He was standing in the clearing, smoking, trying his best to look casual. Ricky stepped into view and asked him for a light. He steadied the guy's hand as he lit his cigarette.

'Quiet night,' Ricky said.

'Yeah.'

'Not much action.'

'No. Very quiet.'

Ricky stretched his arms above his head, his tee shirt riding up just enough to reveal his flat, toned stomach.

'You wanna go back to my place?' the guy asked.

'Is it far?'

'Ten minutes.'

The car park was deserted, except for a dark blue Mercedes Sports. Ricky slid into the passenger seat. The car had the tarry scent of new leather.

'Nice wheels,' Ricky said.

'I've only just bought it,' the guy told him. 'It handles well.'

'You must be well off.'

'I do okay.'

'Do you live on your own?'

'I live with Charlie.' The guy winked. 'He's out exercising at the moment.'

The guy placed a hand on Ricky's thigh, then moved it a little higher. Ricky tensed and pushed the hand away.

'Wait until we get to your place.'

The guy sighed and turned the key in the ignition.

'By the way,' Ricky said, 'I've got a present for you.' He struck the guy hard on the chin, snapping his head sideways with the force of the blow. He punched him again, his fist connecting with the back of his skull, and the guy slumped forward onto the steering wheel. Ricky pulled him up by his hair and slapped his cheek a couple of times. He was out cold.

'Night night, sweetheart.'

Ricky found the guy's wallet: fifty pounds in cash, a gym membership, a couple of credit cards, a Barclays debit card and a driving licence. He checked the details: *Paul Webster, 1 Farm Lane, Lambourne End.*

He dumped Paul Webster unceremoniously in the boot of the car, pocketed the wallet and got behind the wheel. Gravel crackled under rubber as he eased into first gear and drove smoothly away.

*

1 Farm Lane was a large, detached house, close to the road with a front drive that must once have been a small garden. Ricky parked up and killed the engine. The house was in darkness. Charlie must still be out. Ricky snatched the bunch of keys from the ignition and tried one in the front door. The door swung open. The hallway was eerie and oppressive. Ricky felt suddenly uneasy. He searched the ground floor for valuables then made his way upstairs. He became aware of a vague musky smell. He was in some kind of junk room: piles of old newspapers dumped on the floor, a mop and bucket, and what looked like a large empty display case.

The bedrooms yielded up an impressive collection of jockstraps, briefs and sex toys but nothing worth stealing. He ignored the bathroom and found the study.

The walls were crammed with film posters, rows

of books and DVDs. Then he saw the computer desk housing a hard drive and monitor: bingo!

Ricky sat down and booted up, sliding out the keyboard as the screen lit up. He took a flash drive from his pocket and inserted it into the USB port. He clicked reboot, folded his arms and sat back. It would be about sixty seconds before he could start hacking into the computer: bank account details, security codes, dirty selfies. Mr Paul Webster's life was about to open up to him.

*

Charlie watched silently from the shadows. He watched the young man preoccupied by the big glowing screen. Things were flashing on the screen. Bright, shiny things. Charlie heard the rapid staccato of the man's fingers on the keyboard. He was bothered by the sound. He moved silently across the floor.

Ricky realised something was moving behind him and froze. Then he turned to see Charlie, about eight feet long, his body pale and powerful. Ricky screamed as Charlie struck, coiling swiftly round Ricky's neck and chest. Ricky pushed and twisted and bucked. His panicked breathing came in short quick gasps. With each breath, Charlie held him tighter, constricting his chest, squeezing the carotid arteries in his neck. The room began to dim. Ricky's body spasmed and juddered, as if orgasming, then went slack. Charlie lay perfectly still, coiled

tightly around Ricky in the warm, dark stillness of
the house.

Image Credits

Cover: Lalesh Aldarwish
https://www.pexels.com/photo/167964/

Out of Water: Cottonbro
https://www.pexels.com/photo/4788107/

Clem: Cottonbro
https://www.pexels.com/photo/4980366/

Children of Sirius: Monstera
https://www.pexels.com/photo/5331098/

Forbidden: Ketut Subiyanto
https://www.pexels.com/photo/4834250/

45 Minutes: Nagy Szabi
https://www.pexels.com/photo/4134204/

Hairy Tale: Zuarav
https://www.pexels.com/photo/2951989/

Expiry Date: Nagy Szabi
https://www.pexels.com/photo/4134204/

Run!: Nappy
https://www.pexels.com/photo/1682826/

My Funny Valentine: Maria Orlova
https://www.pexels.com/photo/4946522/

The Muddlers: Hamid Tajik
https://www.pexels.com/photo/546533o

Possession: Kindel Media
https://www.pexels.com/photo/7773260/

New, Improved: Cottonbro
https://www.pexels.com/photo/7671469/

Prowler: Erme Keshavarz
https://www.pexels.com/photo/5156489/

The Swedish House: Cottonbro
https://www.pexels.com/photo/5435560/

Echoes: Griffin Wooldridge
https://www.pexels.com/photo/2676582

Charlie: Dontay Sandwich
https://www.pexels.com/photo/2537951

9 781912 622337